MW00584245

Japanese Tales
of Lafcadio Hearn

ODDLY MODERN FAIRY TALES
Jack Zipes, *Series Editor*

Oddly Modern Fairy Tales is a series dedicated to publishing unusual literary fairy tales produced mainly during the first half of the twentieth century. International in scope, the series includes new translations, surprising and unexpected tales by well-known writers and artists, and uncanny stories by gifted yet neglected authors. Postmodern before their time, the tales in *Oddly Modern Fairy Tales* transformed the genre and still strike a chord.

Japanese Tales
of Lafcadio Hearn

Edited and introduced by Andrei Codrescu

With a foreword by Jack Zipes

PRINCETON UNIVERSITY PRESS *Princeton and Oxford*

Copyright © 2019 by Princeton University Press

All illustrations in this book except figure 1: Rare Book Division, Department of Rare Books and Special Collections, Princeton University Library. These are black-and-white versions of color illustrations by Yasumasa Fujita from an edition of *Kwaidan*, by Lafcadio Hearn, printed in 1932 for members of The Limited Editions Club by The Shimbi Shoin, Ltd., Tokyo, Japan.

Figure 1 is a photograph of Lafcadio Hearn from the Miriam and Ira D. Wallach Division of Art, Prints and Photographs: Print Collection, The New York Public Library. "Lafcadio Hearn." New York Public Library Digital Collections.

Published by Princeton University Press
41 William Street, Princeton, New Jersey 08540
6 Oxford Street, Woodstock, Oxfordshire OX20 1TR

press.princeton.edu

All Rights Reserved

LCCN 2018952835
ISBN (pbk.) 978-0-691-16775-6

British Library Cataloging-in-Publication Data is available

Editorial: Anne Savarese and Thalia Leaf
Production Editorial: Sara Lerner
Text Design: Pamela Schnitter
Cover Design: Jessica Massabrook
Cover Credit: Cover illustration by Andrea Dezsö
Production: Erin Suydam
Publicity: Jodi Price and Katie Lewis
Copyeditor: Jennifer Harris

This book has been composed in Adobe Jenson and Myraid

Printed on acid-free paper. ∞

Printed in the United States of America

10 9 8 7 6 5 4 3 2 1

■ Contents

From *Kwaidan: Stories and Studies of Strange Things* (1904)

Out of the blending of the stern sense of impermanence and karma with the sensuous beauty of Japan there arises this new feeling of the weird. . . . Had it been that Mr. Hearn's art sufficed only to reproduce the delicacy and the ghostliness of Japanese tales, he would have performed a notable but scarcely an extraordinary service to letters. But into the study of these by ways of Oriental literature he has carried a third element, the dominant idea of Occidental science; and this element he has blended with Hindu religion and Japanese aestheticism in a combination as bewildering as it is voluptuous. In this triple union lies his real claim to high originality.

—PAUL ELMER MOORE, *Atlantic Monthly* (1902)

As Andrei Codrescu demonstrates in his incisive analysis of Lafcadio Hearn's life and work, there is no better adjective than "weird" to describe what Hearn did and what happened to him. Nothing appears to make sense in his life, and yet, everything has its sense. Hearn spent his life creating and collecting stories from the margins of the societies in which he lived in an effort to find a place to which he could belong. No matter how different these societies were, Hearn was always drawn to their weird aspects. As he stated in a letter written to his friend, the writer William Douglas O'Connor: "I think a man must devote himself to one thing in order to succeed: so I have pledged me to the worship of the Odd, the Queer, the Strange, the Exotic, the Monstrous. . . . Enormous and lurid facts are certainly worthy of more artistic study than they generally receive."[1]

It was not until 1890, however, that Hearn could finally realize his "pledge"—a devotion to Japanese culture in all its aspects. In his introduction, Codrescu reveals the difficult phases of Hearn's life from the tiny Greek island Lefkada to Ireland, London, Cincinnati, New Orleans, and finally to Japan, where he became "mythic." As Codrescu writes:

> Hearn's existential, intellectual, and literary adventures in the living world, were, in the end, a spiral, not circular journey. He never returned to the womb of his mother's Lefkada but found himself at home in a patriarchal world where he was a Father, unlike his own genitor. The critical tools for the "enigma" of Hearn, as critics and biographers are fond of repeating, are still insufficient for the wealth of forms and content that Hearn produced. Hearn was loved by readers who were not concerned with the enigma. They consumed his writing in a manner one might call postmodern, like films or mysteries, and if they thought of it critically, they would have described him and his work as "exotic" and "strange." He was that, in the same manner that fairy tales and fantastic stories are exotic and strange. . . . Lafcadio Hearn lived many lives, experienced miraculous encounters, overcame numerous dragons, and triumphed in the end. His life resembled a fairy tale, but far from ending like some fairy tales do, with disintegration into dust due to a sudden attack of nostalgia, Hearn did not succumb to the temptation to look backward and grew into a myth for the people of Japan, his last place of wandering.

Since it is virtually impossible to capture the manner in which Hearn conveyed a weird sense and atmosphere in the Japanese tales that he translated, adapted, and re-created, Codrescu has collected some of Hearn's most poignant stories from four major works: *Out of the East: Reveries and Studies in New Japan* (1897), *Shadowings* (1900), *A Japanese Miscellany: Strange Stories, Folklore Gleanings, Studies Here & There* (1901), and *Kwaidan: Stories and Studies of Strange Things* (1904). All of the stories have a unique hybrid quality to them. Though they were based on Japanese legends, myths, and fairy tales, Hearn took great poetic license and honed them into weird narratives. They cannot be considered authentic Japanese tales: they are estranged from Japanese tradition in the way that Bertolt Brecht used the estrangement effect in the theater. Hearn sought to stun readers by intensifying the unpredictable in life so that they would question the accepted social norms in Western and Eastern societies at the same time. He honed and changed the Japanese stories he retold for two audiences while at the same time providing factual notes about places, people, and history. The footnotes and commentary with the texts make the tales seem more realistic and yet allow for departures from reality. Chance, death, diverse gods, and reincarnation haunt Hearn's literary versions of Japanese oral and literary works. Endings are rarely happy. Instead they unseat readers, especially those accustomed to the traditional happy endings of Western fairy tales.

Codrescu's introduction to the present anthology clarifies how Hearn, who had a prodigious knowledge of Japanese folklore, developed a surrealist fairy-tale style that was terse and multifaceted. There was no writer like Hearn in his day, and his oddly modern fairy tales still hold great appeal for readers accustomed to the postmodern narratives of our own time. —JACK ZIPES

Note

1. Elizabeth Bisland, *The Life and Letters of Lafcadio Hearn*, vol. 1 (Boston: Houghton Mifflin, 1906): 328–329. This letter was written on June 29, 1884.

Japanese Tales
of Lafcadio Hearn

Lafcadio Hearn, the Ghost of Islands

At the end of the nineteenth century, Lafcadio Hearn was one of America's best known writers, one of a stellar company that included Mark Twain, Edgar Allan Poe, and Robert Louis Stevenson. Twain, Poe, and Stevenson have entered the established literary canon and are still read for duty and pleasure. Lafacadio Hearn has been forgotten, with two remarkable exceptions: in Louisiana and in Japan. Yet Hearn's place in the canon is significant for many reasons, not least of which is how the twentieth century came to view the nineteenth. This view, both academic and popular, reflects the triumph of a certain futuristic modernism over the mysteries of religion, folklore, and what was once called "folk wisdom." To witness this phenomenon in time-lapse, sped-up motion, one need only consider Lafcadio Hearn, the Greek-born, Irish-raised, New World immigrant who metamorphosed from a celebrated fin-de-siècle American writer into the beloved Japanese cultural icon Koizumi Yakumo in less than a decade, in roughly the same time that Japan changed from a millennia-old feudal society into a great industrial power. In other words, in the blink of an eye, in the time it takes a princess to kiss-turn a frog into a prince, or in the time it takes to burn an owl's feathers so that only the nocturnal beautiful-girl-shape of the creature might remain.

History is a fairy tale true to its telling. Lafcadio Hearn's lives are a fairy tale true in various tellings, primarily his own, then those of his correspondents, and with greater uncertainty, those of his biographers. Hearn changed, as if magically, from one person into another, from a Greek islander into a British student, from a penniless London street ragamuffin into a respected American newspaper writer, from a journalist into a novelist, and, most astonishingly, from a stateless Western man into a loyal Japanese citizen. His sheer number of guises make him a creature of legend, by far more fabulous than a frog turning into a prince. Yet this life, as recorded both by himself and by others, grows more mysterious the more one examines it, for it is like the Japanese story of the Buddhist monk Kwashin Koji, in "Impressions of Japan," who owned a painting so detailed it flowed with life. A samurai chieftain saw it and wanted to buy it, but the monk wouldn't sell it, so the chieftain had him followed and murdered. But when the painting was brought to the chieftain and unrolled, there was nothing on it; it was blank. Hearn reported this story told to him by a Japanese monk[1] to illustrate some aspect of the Buddhist doctrine of karma, but he might as well have been speaking about himself as Koji: the more "literary" the renderings of the original story, the less fresh and vivid it becomes, until it might literally disappear, like that legendary painting.

The knowable tellings of Hearn are particular, interesting, and specific to the literary personae of Lafcadio-Koizumi, insofar as one is absorbed and lost in them. But this tremendously prolific producer of literature remains, somehow, elusive. Hearn tempts, or we could say "dares," his critics to interpret his work and his life, but, in the end, he belongs to the reader who best surrenders to his stories and his own life-reporting.

Lafcadio Hearn was born in 1850 not far from Ithaca, on the island of Lefkada in Greece, from the union of Charles Bush Hearn, an Irish surgeon in the British army, and Rosa Kassimatis, a beautiful Greek woman born on Cythera, Aphrodite's island, about which Baudelaire wrote (in Richard Howard's memorable translation): "On Aphrodite's island all I found / was a token gallows wherein my image hung."[2] Hearn's sorrows later in life were reflected by Baudelaire, who saw in Cythera the fatal beauty that would haunt Hearn's life. Lafcadio Hearn was named after Lefkada, where he lived with his mother, while his father was deployed by the British army elsewhere. The island of Lefkada, said by Ovid in his "Ode to Love" to be the place where Sappho jumped to her death in the sea because of unrequited love, was Lafcadio's paradise, the womb-island from which he was "expelled" when his father returned and took mother and child to Dublin. On that dismal northern isle, Lafcadio was expelled a second time, this time away from his mother. While his father was abroad on yet another military assignment in the West Indies, Rosa fled Dublin with a Greek man, back to her "island of feasting hearts and secret joys,"[3] leaving Lafcadio in the custody of a pious Catholic aunt. Then a schoolyard accident in one of the British schools he resentfully attended left him blind in one eye. His father remarried, and his aunt's family became bankrupt, two unrelated yet near-simultaneous disasters. A seventeen-year-old Lafcadio wandered penniless in London among vagabonds, thieves, and prostitutes. In the spring of 1869, a relation of his father's, worried about the family's reputation, handed him a one-way boat ticket to the United States, then overland to Cincinnati, Ohio, where another relation of the Hearns lived.

His departure for the New World was Lafacadio Hearn's third exile. In Cincinnati, where he had imagined generous help, his relation handed him a few dollars and told him to fend for himself. A twenty-year-old Lafcadio found himself, once again, a penniless tramp. So far, with the exception of a few school exercises and some ghoulish poetry inspired by his fear of ghosts, Lafcadio Hearn had written nothing. In Cincinnati, he lived again in the underworld, until a kind angel intervened: the printer Henry Watkin allowed the young tramp to sleep on piles of old newspapers in his shop. Watkin, a utopian anarchist, encouraged the youth to read radical and fantastic literature. It was the age of socialism, anarchism, imperialism, untaxed wealth, unredeemable poverty, spiritism, snake-oil, newspapers, electricity, photography, telegraphy, telepathy, railroads, high art, and kitsch. A bounty of exotic objects and customs flowed in from the cultures of vanquished Native American tribes and recently freed African slaves. The astonished masses of immigrant Europeans, who were mostly peasants and religiously persecuted marginals, brought with them their own rich stories of folklore, customs, and beliefs. Hearn, like many new Americans, felt rightly that he was living in a time of wonder and possibility. His education took a vast leap: he underwent a kind of osmosis as if he had absorbed the spirit of nineteenth-century America from the very newspapers he slept on. He had lived variously and wanted to let the world know how cruel and wondrous life was. Clumsily, with Henry Watkin's encouragement, he started to write.

He submitted a story to the *Enquirer*, a failing yellow-press daily. His story appeared in bold type on the front page. Other stories soon followed. Young Hearn's first writings were blood-curdling reportage steeped in gothic horror. His reports about gruesome murders and exposés of German slaughterhouses in Cincinnati are still cringe-worthy. They scandalized the readers of the *Enquirer* and lifted the newspaper from near-bankruptcy to a prosperous business. Hearn's ultra-realist exposés were drenched in the wounded sensibility of a writer with a merciless eye who had Greek myths and Celtic fairy tales in his blood.

Here he is, describing the murdered body of one Herman Schilling, boiled to death by two of his slaughterhouse confederates: "The brain had all but boiled away, save a small wasted lump at the base of the skull about the size of a lemon. It was crisped and still warm to the touch. On pushing the finger through the crisp, the interior felt about the consistency of banana fruit, and the yellow fibers seemed to writhe like worms in the Coroner's hands. The eyes were cooked to bubbled crisps in the blackened sockets."[4]

For all its facticity, the passage feels like the elaboration of horror in a fairy tale by a storyteller scaring children around a campfire. Young Hearn is telling a story for an audience safely snuggled in the parlor of a Victorian home, usually lit by gas lamps, but candlelit for the occasion. The vivid prose of his newspaper crime-writing was soon employed in no-less-vivid accounts of life on the other side of the tracks, in the Black Quarter, where a different life, language, and time prevailed. Hearn noted the sounds of nightlife, the slang of dockworkers, the rhythms of the street, the strength of language of an underclass whose existence was barely acknowledged or, until then, completely ignored by readers of the *Enquirer*. Hearn wrote passionately about the rough experiences and traumatic lives of his friends and acquaintances.

At the height of his Cincinnati success as a journalist, gossip about his personal life undermined his standing. His stories about the misery and magic of the city's underworld started upsetting the upstanding citizens, who had seen them, to a point, as mere fancies. A *pur sang* bohemian, Hearn lived in a world far from his bourgeois readers. He is said to have married a black woman and lived with her on the other side of the tracks: a scandal in the segregated city. The *Enquirer* fired him.

Spurning offers from rival newspapers, Hearn abandoned Cincinnati and departed for New Orleans, a Creole city of complex race relations, riotous living, legends, conspiracies, public secrets, and voodoo rites. New Orleans was a city in exile from mainstream America, and New Orleans loved Lafcadio Hearn at first reading. From his early columns in the local newspapers to his novel *Chita*, his literary persona took on mythic proportions. In New Orleans, he did not have to hide his commutes between the demimonde of the French Quarter and respectable Uptown. The wealthy citizenry of Uptown enjoyed many of the favors of the French Quarter. Hearn's love of the fantastic, the ghostly, and the outlandish found fertile ground. His path had been paved already by the eccentric and surrealist fiction of Baron von Reizenstein, a German radical refugee, who had transformed the city into a metropolis of the uncanny through his daily serial novel "The Mysteries of New Orleans." The form of "The Mysteries" was well known to German immigrants, who read such tales serialized in German-language newspapers in several of their cities of immigration, most notably Cleveland and New Orleans. The Baron outdid them all by inventing a speciae of journalism that was accurate enough for the daily newspaper he published himself (in German) in New Orleans; his taste for the fantastic featured thousand-year-old vampires frolicking with pedophile priests, lesbian voodoo priestesses (a first in American literature), blacks, adventurers of many shades and scams, faux-aristocrats, assassins, and sinister strangers who floated down the Mississippi River toward the Gulf of Mexico. Von Reizenstein's oeuvre was the centerpiece of an ephemeral literature of illustrated pamphlets about sensational crimes, newspaper exposés of corrupt politicians, "blue books" advertising the establishments in the red light district of Storyville, and spontaneous literature published during epidemics and natural disasters. At the same time, earnest scholars conducted research in Creole customs, legends, language, and the city's history. Writers holding tables in sidewalk cafes attempted to reach Romantic literary heights, their prose like overripe mangoes.

The steamy tropical embrace of New Orleans emboldened the young Hearn to heighten his own language for impressionist effects. And he made literary friendships. His new friends, the journalist Elizabeth Bisland, the novelist George Washington Cable (Mark Twain's touring companion), and Père de la Rouquette (Catholic priest, poet, scholar of Creole and Choctaw, author of the first Louisiana history), encouraged the young writer to study Creole and Cajun folklore, and to transcribe the stories and chants of the voudouins. They speculated about Eastern philosophies, occult texts, and rituals. Hearn's colorful newspaper essays about local lore, his articles about high and low New Orleans life, and his translations from the French of Gautier, Maupassant, and Loti drew many admirers. His reputation grew. While writing for the New Orleans papers, he attracted the attention of New York literati and was courted by major publishers. He started writing for *Harper's Weekly* and published his first book, *Chita, a Memory of Last Island*, with Harper and Brothers. The novella, set on Grand Isle, the favorite vacation refuge of New Orleanians fleeing the unhealthy summer of the city, remains one of the classics of Louisiana literature and has never gone out of print. The Louisiana coast, always under the threat of vanishing, found in Hearn the perfect chronicler of its vaporous tenure and its intensely emotional people.

In Hearn's old London house of misery, like elsewhere in Europe, the social visions of Charles Fourier, Marx, and Baudelaire, and the otherworldly imaginings of gothic writers, were undermining the traditional order. In America, communities inspired by those ideas began to embody alternatives. Hearn's bohemia was a disorderly experiment, but others, like the Oneida commune in New York, founded on the idea of free love, were practical extensions of the European social and literary revolution. Hearn considered joining Oneida (inspired by his Fourierist host and mentor, Henry Watkin), but the company of handsome Anglo-Saxon specimens assembled by the community's founder, John Humphrey Noyes, had no room in it for the dwarfish, one-eyed, mixed-race Hearn. His home was in language, and his imagination made a place for him in the sea of the magical stories he discovered in New Orleans. Hearn was lost, sent into permanent exile by his genitors, an inhabitant, par excellence, of the Outside. America was itself a refuge for outsiders, and New Orleans was in many ways outside America. Having literally lived outside and fought inclement weather and hunger with a classless underworld, Hearn was a dreamer with a vengeance and a merciless observer of humans. And he was, for the moment, a literary sensation.

In 1887, Hearn departed for the West Indies on assignment for *Harper's Weekly*, unconsciously following the path of his father, the military surgeon deployed there by the British army. The younger Hearn set off for the island of Martinique, "with ports of call at St. Croix, St. Kitts, Montserrat, Barbados, Trinidad, Tobago, St. Lucia, and British Guiana."[5] He lived in Martinique for two years, fully immersed in island life, writing detailed notes on its people, its foods, its lush flora, and its vertiginous landscapes. His descriptions of the *porteuses*, the strong and graceful women who ran the length and width of the island's mountainous roads carrying tremendous weights of merchandise on their heads, is preserved forever in his book *Two Years in the French West Indies*, as is the capital city of St. Pierre, which was completely destroyed by the eruption of the Mount Pelée volcano in 1902.[6] In this book, published in 1889, Hearn's prose reached both its Victorian apogee and a sharpness of detail that prefigured the modern taste for precise observation. The decorative filler for the newspapers began to lose its charms for Hearn. He yearned for something simpler and sturdier, a wish for an unadorned style that he would later seek in Japan.

In his introduction to *The Selected Writings of Lafcadio Hearn*[7] (1949), the editor Malcolm Cowley was by turns critical and complimentary. He found Hearn's writing for newspapers in Cincinnati and New Orleans guilty of "a purple style." (The same can be said of Hearn's translations from the French of Theophile Gautier and Pierre Loti.) Of Hearn's New Orleans novels, *Chita* and *Youma*, Cowley said, "the atmosphere is more important than the story." Cowley's view of the young Hearn's prolific output echoes that of the subject himself, who wrote from Japan in 1893 to his friend Basil Chamberlain, who had returned to Europe: "After for years studying poetical prose, I am forced now to study simplicity. After attempting my utmost at ornamentation, I am converted by my own mistakes. The great point is to touch with simple words."[8] In the end, Cowley thought that Hearn found his subject in Japan, as well as his identity in Koizumi Yakumo, the name he adopted later in life. In other words, Hearn had completed an epic journey in search of himself, a circular odyssey in both real-time and word-time, as adventure-filled as that of Odysseus and perhaps Homer, but which was not a return to the island where he was born, though it had taken him from one island to another.

Commissioned by *Harper's* to write a series of reports similar to his *Two Years in the French West Indies*, Hearn arrived in Yokohama on April 2, 1890, only a few decades after the first American warship commanded by Commodore Perry arrived, under orders from President Millard Fillmore, to open Japanese ports to American trade. The American incursion caused the defeat of Tokugawa, the last anti-Western shogun, the restoration of the emperor, and the beginning of rapid industrialization in Meiji Japan. It was an era of endings and beginnings, tailor-made to Hearn's philosophical and literary questions, which coincided with the very moment that a traditional and deeply ritual-based culture was experiencing a violent break with its past and an accelerated jump into the future. No stranger to violent breaks and accelerated leaps, Hearn would find himself choosing without hesitation the mythical past—patriarchal samurai Japan.

Lafcadio's Japanese life began in typically inauspicious fashion when his few contacts promised to find him a job and didn't. The money vaguely promised by *Harper's Weekly* for his reports from Japan never showed up. One of his contacts, who would, like Elizabeth Bisland, become a lifelong friend and correspondent, Professor Basil Hall, chamberlain of Tokyo University, advised him to write down his first impressions of Japan as soon as he experienced them. It was sound advice; it allowed Hearn to communicate the overwhelming sensations of an exotic world to American readers, a world that conformed to their expectations of miniature people, paper houses, decorated streets, spectacular views of Mount Fuji, and Buddhist temples where one might conduct long philosophical talks with Buddhist monks. For Hearn, who would go on to write twelve major books in Japan, one of the most startling and illuminating insights came early. Wondering about the *ghostly* sensation of Japanese art, he concluded that it is due to

> the absence of shadows. What prevents you from missing them at once is the astounding skill in the recognition and use of color-values. The scene . . . is not depicted as if illumined from one side, but as if throughout suffused with light. . . . The old Japanese loved shadows made by the moon, and painted the same, but these were weird and did not interfere with color. But they had no admiration for shadows that blacken and break the charm of the world under the sun. And the inner as well as the outer world was luminous for them. Psychologically also they saw life without shadows. Then the West burst into their Buddhist peace, and saw their art and bought it all up . . . and when there was nothing more to be bought, and it seemed possible that fresh creation might reduce the market price of what had been bought already, then the West said: "Oh, come now! you mustn't go on drawing and seeing things that way, you know. It isn't Art! You must really learn to see shadows, you know—and pay me to teach you." So Japan paid to learn how to see shadows in Nature, in life, and in thought.[9]

This reflection contains Hearn's lifelong concern with shadows (one of his Japanese books is *Shadowings*, published by Little, Brown in 1900), his naïve, self-generated enthusiasm in all new places seen in the light of a return to paradise, and an important aesthetic that saw religious symbolism and art as one. The West, viewed in terms of greed, concupiscence, and the villainy of money, corrupted the spiritual life of people not yet converted by the "market" by introducing the shadows of death. Death and its shadows preoccupied Hearn his entire life, but they took new meaning in Japan, where death was a starkly defined world. The ghostly world, the activities of the dead, the influence of the dead on the living, the complex Buddhist teachings about death, are in almost every one of Hearn's essays, but are most present in his rendering of Japanese fairy tales, where he found the stories in the abstract Buddhist concepts. These stories were the folk translations of the Buddhist monks and scholars' explanations. They contained the charm and thrill of a mysterious world. Otherworldly mysteries as told by the common folk always interested Hearn and fascinated his readers. In the rich lore of Japanese stories, many of which were told to him by his second wife, Setsu, Hearn found the revelation that death as introduced to Japan by Western ideas was corrupting the Buddhist teachings on death and the afterlife. Hearn's early insight was later developed in the essays of Ernest Fenollosa, a historian of Japanese art and a professor of philosophy at the University of Tokyo. Ezra Pound, the founder of American modernist poetry, took Fenollosa's thought further and influenced poets throughout the twentieth century. Hearn's insight was influenced by the English philosopher Herbert Spencer, whose books were responsible for much of Hearn's "spiritual" education under Watkin's tutelage. In addition to the high-minded Spencer, Hearn was fascinated by occult experiments and was an avid reader of the prodigious and quarrelsome Madame Blavatsky, who claimed to have been taught by Buddhist masters during her trances and dreams.

Despite such insights, Hearn's early writings in Japan evinced little of the search for the "simplicity" that he confessed to

Chamberlain. They instead conformed to the exotic expectations of American readers. What makes his early Japanese observations a cut above the era's conventional travel writings are the anecdotes he collected and transcribed from his conversations with Buddhist monks, as well as from ordinary people he met in daily life. In answers to Hearn's lofty question about life and death, one monk told him "Buddhism teaches that all sexual love must be suppressed . . . as necessity or hindrance to enlightenment"—not exactly what Hearn meant, but perhaps what he really wanted to hear. An eighty-eight-year-old Zen priest told him a story about a celibate monk who was a "comely man" of whom a girl became enamored. She grieved in secret about the impossibility of breaching her beloved's vows, until in the thrall of her passion she went to Lord Buddha himself to speak her heart, whereupon Lord Buddha cast her in a deep sleep. She dreamed that she was the happy wife of her beloved. After many years of contentment and sorrow in her dream, her husband died. She was wracked by unbearable pain, and in the midst of it she woke up and saw Buddha smile. "'You have a choice,' Buddha told her. 'You can either be a bride, or seek his Higher way.' Then she cut her hair, and became a nun, and in aftertime attained to the condition of one never to be reborn."[10] Hearn was lonely, and such edifying tales were not lost on him. He was looking for a companion.

By the gracious fortune that never failed him, Hearn eventually obtained a modest position teaching English in the city of Matsue, hundreds of miles away from Tokyo. In Matsue, old Japan was still faithful to its samurai past; its ceremonies, festivals, manners, and rigid class distinctions were scrupulously observed. Hearn felt that in this traditional and self-contained world he was no odder than any other Westerner: his modest height was only slightly more than that of the average Japanese man, and his odd appearance was naturally that of a foreigner. His students liked him and showed him the deference due to respected elders. An exhausted Lafcadio Hearn, worn out by late nights in the ill-famed quarters of cities, and the strain of incessantly writing with one overworked eye for the insatiable publications that earned him a meager living, found the slow ritual pace of Matsue a delight. Approached by a colleague who proposed that he marry a young Japanese woman from an impoverished but noble samurai family, he eagerly agreed. His marriage would be considered an act of compassion toward her family, which he would be obligated to support in exchange for surrendering their daughter, Setsu. Lafcadio's teacher's salary was high by local standards, and he could easily afford his married responsibilities. In January 1891, the twenty-fourth year of Meiji, he celebrated his nuptials with Setsu Koizumi with rice wine in the presence of friends. Setsu was unschooled, but she was an intelligent and attentive woman who held a treasury of old folk stories, legends, and ghost tales in her memory. She was also a traditional Japanese woman who had been trained to obey all of her husband's wishes and show him great respect. In the newlyweds' traditional house, Setsu and their servants stood to bow when he left for his job and did the same when he returned. Custom dictated that he eat first, before the others in the household, and that he remain unbothered in his occupations. Lafcadio Hearn had hit the jackpot. He put on his Japanese robe, sat on his straw mat, and applied himself to the task of becoming Japanese.

In a letter to Basil Chamberlain on October 11, 1893, he described the feeling: "at home I enter into my little smiling world of old ways and thoughts and courtesies;—where all is soft and gentle as something seen in sleep. It is so soft, so intangibly gentle and lovable and artless, that sometimes it seems a dream only; and then a fear comes that it might vanish away. It has become Me. When I am pleased, it laughs; when I don't feel jolly, everything is silent. I cannot imagine what I should do away from it."

Here, in a nutshell, is the fairy tale of Lafcadio Hearn's life in Japan, lit by the magic lamp of wish. But in order to make it just so, Hearn had work to do, the hardest of which was to cease being Lafcadio Hearn. Since he had at first seen himself primarily as an American writer explaining Japan to the West, he would have to teach himself to think differently, to begin achieving that "artless" art that disallowed such phrases as "soft, so intangibly gentle as something seen in sleep." The Victorian ornamentation had to go. The overwrought newspaper writing had to go. The object had to be lit only by the fact of it, which worded simply contained all that needed to be said.

It took time. Having specialized in nightmares as a writer, "intangible gentleness" would have rarely entered his sleep. Yet this intangible gentleness was the undergirding of his child-dream of the womb of Lefkada, and he was far from it yet. Still connected to New York publishers, an indefatigable writer of letters to his friends, moved by a compulsive need to compare "West" and "East," Hearn had many selves invested in getting at that elusive "intangible." His letters to his American friends are self-consciously literary and conscious also of their readers. To Elizabeth Bisland, he wrote warmly but "properly," with only hints of his shadowy adventures, despite their wild past in New Orleans. Bisland, in the two-volume biography of Hearn that she published two years after his death, defended him from his "scandalous reputation," especially since it involved her own life, which had become quite puritanical in her New York milieu. In his first letters to Chamberlain, Hearn sounded quite a bit more scholarly and philosophical, showing off his reading and research. Later, when they knew each other better, there is considerable ease and even a dirty joke (elegantly phrased) here and there. The correspondents also shared a growing exasperation at discovering that although the Japanese are guarded and wear many masks required by society and tradition, under these reside the same vicissitudes of human nature present everywhere. Only to his mentor and friend, the anarchist printer Henry Watkin, did Hearn reveal himself in rowdy and unfettered form, and it is in these letters (selected in most editions of *Letters from the Raven*[11]) that we see the transformation he was indeed undergoing, from gothic writer and adventurer to a traditional paterfamilias and a serious student of Japanese lore.

Setsu was a patient companion and teacher. She gave him four children, whom Lafcadio loved, especially his son Kazuo, who became a teacher of English and wrote a book about his father.[12] Setsu taught Lafcadio stories and songs and helped improve his speech as he learned Japanese. She saw to it that his unpredictable moods were understood and protected by the family that filled his life. The "bohemian by necessity," as Cowley calls him, became a man who dedicated himself to the education of children, his own and others', an assiduous student, and a fervent defender of old Japan against what he saw as the corruption of the West. In February 1896, Lafcadio Hearn became the Japanese citizen Yakumo Koizumi. Adopted by his Japanese family as a condition for citizenship, he took the family name Koizumi, meaning "little spring", and chose for his own name Yakumo, meaning "eight clouds," which was the first word of the "most ancient poem extant in the Japanese language," as well as one of the names for Izumo, "my beloved province, the place of the Issuing of the Clouds."

Hearn set himself to the task of studying and translating haiku and tanka, forms of Japanese poetry that made brevity their virtue; his meditations on these forms and the economy they entailed echoed for Ernest Fenollosa (who was living in Japan and invited Hearn to visit, an invitation Hearn testily refused), and Ezra Pound. His insights had an even longer life through Kenneth Rexroth, who edited a collection of Hearn's Buddhist writings, and Gary Snyder, and they continued to be important to poets. Poetry for every occasion, composed spontaneously, solemn or raucous, was part of Japanese life, and a delight for all ages. Folk poetry, the recitation of epics, provided the threads that Hearn seized on when he wrote *Kwaidan*,[13] his first truly Japanese book written in his best English. It was published in 1904, the year of his death.

Everything that might delight a reader in search of Japanese legends, rituals, and beliefs, whether of Shintō or Buddhist origin—the enchantment of the Japanese imaginary, wisdom about nature (which revolves most often around the cherry tree, Japan's true axis mundi), the feminine forces that rule the universe (certainly Hearn's magical world), and the many shapes of death and afterlife through animals and spirits—can be found in *Kwaidan*. Distilled here are Hearn's efforts to find the forms best suited to his multifaceted personalities: his own masks are to be found here, discarded, haunting, or preserved. *Kwaidan* achieved what Hearn intended to find in Japanese culture: a flowing mix of folk tales, personal observations, and a marvelous series of essays on insects—it is the work of Hearn-Koizumi, a writer with a double vision, an English-language writer deeply intimate with Japan, or a Japanese storyteller consciously writing in English. I have selected most of the stories from *Kwaidan* in this anthology because this is, as most of his readers in the United States and Japan (where it appeared in numerous translations) believe, Hearn's most successful book. In addition, I have included other notable tales from *Shadowings* and *A Japanese Miscellany* that reflect the restrained style and strange incidents that one might think weird and yet significant in Japanese culture.

Before *Kwaidan*, Hearn experimented with many forms of stories: autobiographical sketches, wisdom-parables, travel writing. Most of his work, disseminated through numerous volumes and editions, is pro-Japanese and anti-Western. They position Hearn-Koizumi as a Japanese writer. In his lifetime, his previous writings, from Cincinnati, New Orleans, and the West Indies, were little known to his Japanese readers. At the same time, because of their intended audience and their having been written in English, his Japanese work influenced American writers well into the twentieth century.

Hearn's existential, intellectual, and literary adventures in the living world, were, in the end, a spiral, not a circular journey. He never returned to the womb of his mother's Lefkada but found himself at home in a patriarchal world where he was a Father, unlike his own genitor. The critical tools for the "enigma" of Hearn, as critics and biographers are fond of repeating, are still insufficient for the wealth of forms and content that Hearn produced. Hearn was loved by readers who were not concerned with the enigma. They consumed his writing in a manner one might call postmodern, like films or mysteries, and if they thought of it critically, they would have described him and his work as "exotic" and "strange." He was that, in the same manner that fairy tales and fantastic stories are exotic and strange. This reader's perspective is exactly right: Lafcadio Hearn lived many lives, experienced miraculous encounters, overcame numerous dragons, and triumphed in the end. His life resembled a fairy tale, but far from ending like some fairy tales do, with disintegration into dust due to a sudden attack of nostalgia, Hearn did not succumb to the temptation to look backward and grew into a myth for the people of Japan, his last place of wandering. His stories are always in print in new editions, illustrated by known artists. Films, Noh plays, music, and ballets were (and are) produced based on his ghost stories.

The difficulty for anthologists, including this one, was how to approach the more than one hundred volumes composed by Lafcadio Hearn, sometimes with help from his friends Chamberlain and Bisland. This difficulty is compounded by the editors of publishing houses that issued editions of Hearn's writings without his consent. There were numerous apocryphal texts, published after his death in 1904, "from the school of . . . ," possible forgeries, and bowdlerized or, conversely, sexualized editions printed by fly-by-night publishers looking for a quick buck. Then there are the volumes of letters to his friends, each of them introduced by book-length explanations. Standing separately from his journalistic stories on Japan, his renderings of fairy tales, his Buddhist studies, his philosophical and sociological essays, his lectures (faithfully transcribed by his Japanese students), there is another body of work, a sizable recasting of his life and writing by his biographers. Hearn biographies appeared shortly after his death. These began with Elizabeth Bisland's two volumes in 1906, and continued well into the present with Jonathan Cott's 1992 *Wandering Ghost: The Odyssey of Lafcadio Hearn*. Some biographies repeated, inaccurately, known stories; others collected ephemera, retellings, new versions of original editions, and even unpublished manuscripts. A true student of Hearn's might spend a good decade uncovering the multiple writings of this multifaceted man. Books titled *Japanese*

Fairy Tales are often folk tales taken from longer texts about spiritual matters, linguistic research, or travel notes. Many of Hearn's "Japanese" tales were said to be literary transcriptions of Setsu's storytelling, but they show also the influence of Greek myths and that of Hans Christian Andersen. Some of the tales came from friends and acquaintances. His friends, including Chamberlain and Bisland, added their own stories to Hearn's. The differing styles and subjects reflect the times when they were published, and the tastes of their editors, including Hearn himself.

An interesting instance of this is "Green Willow," a story issuing from the same folk source, but retold by two writers, only one of whom may be Hearn. In the story that is "not Hearn," but also bearing the same title, the later "Green Willow,"[14] the young samurai Tomotada is "a courtier, and a poet, who had a sweet voice and a beautiful face, a noble form," and "was a graceful dancer, and excellent in every manly sport." He is asked by his master, Lord Noto, if he is loyal, and he confirms his loyalty. He is then asked by Lord Noto: "Do you love me?" This, too, is answered with an unhesitant yes. Thus tested, he is sent by his master to carry out a mysterious mission. He is not told what it is, but is given stern warnings of the dangers awaiting him, including that of looking "a maiden in the eyes." Tomotada overcomes many obstacles, but in a cottage in front of which stand three weeping willows, he forgets his master's last warning and falls in love with a beautiful girl, whom he marries. He lives with her in a lovely house and is happy, forgetting all about Lord Noto. After three years, she suddenly dies, with an exclamation: "'The tree,' she moaned, 'the tree. They have cut down the tree. Remember the Green Willow?'" The name of his beloved comes from one of the three weeping willows that stood in front of the cottage where he had met her. After she dies, Tomotada returns to the cottage, and sees that all three willows have been cut down.

It is a tale as mysterious as the unspoken mission: the young samurai is as beautiful as a girl, and he is asked by his master if he loves him. He loves a beautiful girl instead and is punished, but the punishment is not swift. He is given three happy years. Green Willow, who is but one of the three weeping willows, is a choice between three kinds of love: she is the love of women. The other two willows that were also cut down represent two other kinds of love, one of the samurai's love for his master, the other the love of the master for the samurai. Not too deeply buried in the samurai code is the understanding that complete fidelity implies a homoerotic bond. The graceful young samurai with girlish good looks and manly bravery has pledged and betrayed the love of his master. He chose the wrong love. Nonetheless, he is granted three years, which in the samurai world is tantamount to forgiveness. One deduces from this that Lord Noto loved his samurai and still hoped for his return, but after three years, when it appeared clear that Tomotada had chosen Green Willow in his stead, he kills all three weeping willows, one of which must have been his own love. All loves, already "weeping," are severed. It would then seem that Tomotada's mission was to find what he truly loves. This story reveals a gentle side of the samurai code. In all other matters, whether justice, manners, or hierarchy, there is little mercy. Love is given here a dispensation reminiscent of the European Renaissance or the courts of Provence with their troubadours and crusaders.

This story is most likely the work of one of the "others" mentioned in the collection's subtitle, possibly Basil Chamberlain. It is not a story written by Lafcadio Hearn, but is nonetheless the work of someone familiar with Japan.

In *Kwaidan*, which is assuredly the work of Hearn, we find the same story, but in a quite different form. The young samurai Tomotada, in the service of Lord Noto, is sent on a private mission to the daimyo of Kyoto, a kinsman of his master. He asks for permission to stop briefly in his journey to pay a visit to his widowed mother. The countryside is covered in snow, and the lost and exhausted Tomotada finds himself before a cottage where willow trees are growing. Inside, an old man and a young girl are warming themselves before "a fire of bamboo splints." Tomotada seduces the girl with verses, and her family (there must have also been an unnamed old woman) gives her to him gladly, accepting no payment. Samurais could not marry without permission of their masters, but Tomotada ignores the custom. Fearing that her beauty might be noticed and reported, Tomotada keeps her hidden in Kyoto, but a servant spots her and reports the matter to the daimyo, who gives orders to have her brought immediately to his palace to enjoy her for himself. Tomotada is powerless, but he manages nonetheless to send his beloved a letter that expresses in twenty-four syllables all his misery and love for her. He is then summoned to the palace. Tomotada is certain that he will be sentenced to death for his daring, but the daimyo gives his permission instead to take the girl back. The twenty-four-syllable poem had apparently saved him, by awakening the daimyo's most delicate nature. The couple lives together happily for five years, until she confesses, when she suddenly becomes deathly ill, that she is a willow tree and that she is being cut down that very moment. Her dying form sinks down "in the strangest way," just like a cut tree.

The differences between the two versions are great. Aside from the details of the meeting, the reasons for eloping, and the number and (non)number of willow trees, this is not a delicate love story. Poetry that can seduce a girl and save her from the cruelty of a master is a commonplace in Japanese culture. Likewise, the law that called for the master to give a servant permission to marry was part of samurai life. Even the surreal ending, in the confession that she is a tree that must die because she is being cut down, is traditional. Human-trees and tree-humans abound in Japanese folklore: the most celebrated is the cherry tree, but many other trees participate in the fate of humans. One could easily assemble an anthology (by Hearn and others) of tree-centered Japanese fairy tales. In *Kwaidan*, where this story first appeared, it is much longer, and in Hearn's earliest Japanese style, he tries to cram in as many "credible" Japanese details as he can, for the edification of the Western reader. There is no intimacy between Lord Noto and his samurai—absolute fidelity is taken for granted. The only "crime" is not asking permission to marry, which is possibly a sly Hearnian reference to "le droit de seigneur."

The writer who produced the later version was different: a psychologist interested in Japanese eroticism, which is ubiquitous in the native folklore. Ironically, the "author" of the first story in *Kwaidan*, Lafcadio himself, had a reputation for sexualized storytelling, while a scholar, like Chamberlain, for instance, above reproach in his scholarly work, was possibly freed by Hearn to render into vernacular what he knew about samurai society. Hearn would have done his best to suppress this knowledge, as indeed he did in the *Kwaidan* version.

"Momotaro," a story loved in Japan, long attributed to Lafcadio Hearn, is not his either; it is most certainly written by someone familiar with Hans Christian Andersen, possibly familiar with Hearn, but completely unfamiliar with Japan. The traditional beginning is that of a European fairy tale, with a few painful crypto-Japanese "signs," such as something called "kimi-dango" (a kind of millet dumpling) and "sayonara" for "goodbye." The rest concerns a child, born from a peach, who attracts an entourage of animals with his "kimi-dango" and vanquishes some ogres whose treasure he steals.

Hearn, even at his most negligent, was consistent in his transcription; his Japanese tales are stark and do not resemble the fairy tales produced by nineteenth-century writers in Europe. Occasionally, for lack of a transition and for touching a chord in his American readers, he invented elements that were closer to the smoky djinns of the *Thousand and One Nights*, or the monsters of Greek myths, but he rarely employed the repetitions familiar to European readers; instead, he translated brief jingles or occasional poems that were traditional in Japanese stories.

The most often quoted rendering of a true Japanese fairy tale by Hearn is the story of "Urashima," which first appears in sketchy form in a letter Hearn wrote to Basil Chamberlain on July 22, 1893; it reappears in his reverie "The Dream of a Summer Day,"[15] and few anthologies of his fantastic works have ignored it. In "Urashima," the beautiful daughter of the Dragon God of the Sea takes the beautiful fisher-boy Urashima to her father's royal palace under the waters, where they live for many happy years, until Urashima is seized by the desire to see his parents one more time. Not heeding the warnings of his wife and the court, he heads back to the surface, where he grows old and disintegrates into a cloud of dust. Understandably, this is the fairy tale that would best describe Lafcadio's life, had he been able to return to Lefkada. "Urashima" is also a universal fairy tale that appears in many cultures, most memorably in the Romanian (and Balkan variants) of "Youth Without Age and Life Without Death," stories about living eternally in a kingdom of youth without end from which nostalgia expels the lucky hero into the arms of Death, who tells him (in the Romanian version): "I almost died myself waiting so long for you." Then Death slaps him and he turns to dust. There is no doubt that Hearn heard this story in Japan, but oddly, this is his least Japanese story. That honor belongs, in my opinion, to the blind master of the *biwa*, a four-stringed lute, in "The Story of Mimi-Nashi-Hōichi."

The blind singer Hōichi lives and is cared for by monks in a Buddhist monastery, where he is honored for his skill in the musical recitation of an epic battle, a performance that takes many days. One night the biwa-master is led by an unseen warrior to a splendid palace, where he performs the beginning of his epic before what he imagines is a great and noble audience. For many nights he is led to this court and brought back to the temple at dawn. The abbot suspects a trap and discovers the singer in a nearby cemetery, where the dead of the ancient battle are buried. The story of Hōichi is possibly Lafcadio Hearn's best "ghost story" from Japan.

A cursory reading of Japanese fairy tales, scattered throughout Hearn's books, would tempt one to call them "ghost stories." Indeed, many collections do just that, and qualify them with an adjective, such as "strange." They are indeed that, but the attention that the Japanese paid to the afterlife was detailed and absorbing. The afterlife was as populous and eventful as life, but its observation from this shore made it eerie, like the negative of an old film that was forbidden to view. This made it fascinating, of course, but it was of particular interest to Hearn because he had been tossed like a coin from one reality to another, and he made the ghost-world one of his lives. If an afterlife followed him, indeed he would have been hard put to recognize the difference. In dreams, which had always been of particular interest to him, the transition was flawless. Hearn's recollections of his dreams, and his interpretations of them, make him a proto-Surrealist. It is odd that he was left out of the Surrealist canon by André Breton, who included Hearn's close kin, Lewis Carroll and Rimbaud. The Surrealists did not, most likely, read his work, because it was popular. Obscurity shadows literature, a protective shield that Hearn, who was actually read in his own time, did not possess. Yet, he was obscure in the most fantastic and ghostly way. Like the famous vanishing details of the stolen painting, Hearn was absorbed by the ghost-world and put to work as its mouthpiece.

When I began this introduction, I had no idea how deeply Lafcadio Hearn had influenced Japanese culture, and recently, through the Internet, our own. Hearn is a transcultural hybrid writer, a multilingual genre-crosser: born in Greece, raised in several countries and languages, a self-taught scholar, a restless adventurer, a hyper-self-conscious translator—a bridge between the nineteenth and twentieth centuries. The twenty-first century may well contain a new life for this writer. What happened in Hearn's journey, from a fabled Greek island through a surging industrial America to a barely Westernized Japan, is a new kind of ghost story. Hearn contributed an auto-hagiography in letters to his literary friends and in personal essays, but he isn't to be found there. The many travails, transformations, and masks that appeared in his re-renderings in English of Japanese fairy tales are also the stories of No One, one of the names of Odysseus.

In "Mujina,"[16] an old merchant traveling at twilight comes upon a noble woman sobbing by the moat of an ancient castle. Fearing that she intends to drown herself, he attempts to console her by laying a hand "lightly" on her shoulder and asking the reason she is weeping. She turns and uncovers her face, hidden until then "behind her sleeve." The man then sees that she has no eyes or nose or mouth—and he screams and runs away. Desperate for human company, he runs until he sees the lantern of a noodle-seller, who inquires about his distress. After telling his story, the merchant looks for compassion in the peddler's face. "'Hé! Was it anything like THIS that she showed you?' cried the soba-man, stroking his own face—which therewith became like unto an Egg. . . . And, simultaneously, the light went out."

In that mirror, which is almost a joke, the shadow is playful, but the faceless future is painful. The Surrealists hovered in Hearn's future shadow—as did the fantasy industry of the virtual.

Notes

1. Lafcadio Hearn, *A Japanese Miscellany* (Boston: Little, Brown, 1901).
2. Charles Baudelaire, "A Voyage to Cythera," in *Les Fleurs du Mal*, trans. Richard Howard (Boston: David R. Godine, 1982).
3. Baudelaire, "A Voyage to Cythera."
4. This Hearn story, headlined "Skull Had Burst Like a Shell," appeared in the *Cincinnati Enquirer*, quoted in Jonathan Cott, *Wandering Ghost: The Odyssey of Lafcadio Hearn* (New York: Knopf, 1992).
5. Cott, *Wandering Ghost*.
6. *Two Years in the French West Indies* (New York: Harper and Brothers, 1890) is the first book by Lafcadio Hearn that I read as preparatory material for a visit to the West Indies in 1995, to interview the poet Aimé Césaire. Hearn's book was immensely helpful, a beautiful and accurate guidebook, still true in its essentials, with only the glaring physical absence of the *porteuses* and St. Pierre, that were nonetheless present in a ghostly way thanks to the vividness of Hearn's portraits of them. The only survivor of the volcanic eruption of Mount Pelée was the sole inhabitant of the city's jail, locked there for drunkenness. I can't help adding that Lafcadio Hearn, in re-creating the poetry of the city, was another witness to its existence, and doubtlessly a more

articulate one than the celebrated drunk who traveled the world after the eruption, telling his story.

7. Lafcadio Hearn, *Kwaidan: Ghost Stories and Strange Tales of Old Japan* (New York: Houghton Mifflin, 1904).

8. Cited by Malcolm Cowley in his introduction to *The Selected Writings of Lafcadio Hearn*, edited by Henry Goodman (New York: Citadel Press, 1949).

9. Lafcadio Hearn, *Out of the East: Reveries and Studies in New Japan* (New York: Houghton Mifflin, 1895).

10. Quoted and recast from Cott, *Wandering Ghost*, 294.

11. D. B. Updike, ed., *Letters from the Raven, Lafcadio Hearn* (Boston: Merrymount Press, 1907).

12. Kazuo Koizumi, *Father and I, Memories of Lafcadio Hearn* (New York: Houghton Mifflin, 1935).

13. Hearn, *Kwaidan*. The title page of this edition reads, "Kwaidan: Stories and Studies of Strange Things; Lafcadio Hearn, Lecturer on English Literature in the Imperial University of Tokyo, Japan (1896–1903), Honorary Member of the Japan Society London." It was published in April 1904, the year of Hearn's death.

14. *Japanese Fairy Tales*, by Lafcadio Hearn and others (New York: Boni and Liveright, 1918).

15. Hearn, *Out of the East*.

16. Hearn, *Kwaidan*.

TALES

■ The Dream of a Summer Day

I

The hotel seemed to me a paradise, and the maids thereof celestial beings. This was because I had just fled away from one of the Open Ports, where I had ventured to seek comfort in a European hotel, supplied with all "modern improvements." To find myself at ease once more in a yukata, seated upon cool, soft matting, waited upon by sweet-voiced girls, and surrounded by things of beauty, was therefore like a redemption from all the sorrows of the nineteenth century. Bamboo shoots and lotus-bulbs were given me for breakfast, and a fan from heaven for a keepsake. The design upon that fan represented only the white rushing burst of one great wave on a beach, and sea-birds shooting in exultation through the blue overhead. But to behold it was worth all the trouble of the journey. It was a glory of light, a thunder of motion, a triumph of sea-wind,—all in one. It made me want to shout when I looked at it.

Between the cedar balcony pillars I could see the course of the pretty gray town following the shore-sweep,—and yellow lazy junks asleep at anchor,—and the opening of the bay between enormous green cliffs,—and beyond it the blaze of summer to the

Editor's Note: The explanatory footnotes that accompany the tales were written by Lafcadio Hearn.

horizon. In that horizon there were mountain shapes faint as old memories. And all things but the gray town, and the yellow junks, and the green cliffs, were blue.

Then a voice softly toned as a wind-bell began to tinkle words of courtesy into my reverie, and broke it; and I perceived that the mistress of the palace had come to thank me for the chadai,* and I prostrated myself before her. She was very young, and more than pleasant to look upon,—like the moth-maidens, like the butterfly-women, of Kunisada. And I thought at once of death;—for the beautiful is sometimes a sorrow of anticipation.

She asked whither I honorably intended to go, that she might order a kuruma for me. And I made answer:—

"To Kumamoto. But the name of your house I much wish to know, that I may always remember it."

"My guest-rooms," she said, "are augustly insignificant, and my maidens honorably rude. But the house is called the House of Urashima. And now I go to order a kuruma."

The music of her voice passed; and I felt enchantment falling all about me,—like the thrilling of a ghostly web. For the name was the name of the story of a song that bewitches men.

II

Once you hear the story, you will never be able to forget it. Every summer when I find myself on the coast,—especially of very soft, still days,—it haunts me most persistently. There are many native versions of it which have been the inspiration for countless works of art. But the most impressive and the most ancient is found in the "Manyefushifu," a collection of poems dating from the fifth

* A little gift of money, always made to a hotel by the guest shortly after his arrival.

to the ninth century. From this ancient version the great scholar Aston translated it into prose, and the great scholar Chamberlain into both prose and verse. But for English readers I think the most charming form of it is Chamberlain's version written for children, in the "Japanese Fairy-Tale Series,"—because of the delicious colored pictures by native artists. With that little book before me, I shall try to tell the legend over again in my own words.

Fourteen hundred and sixteen years ago, the fisher-boy Urashima Tarō left the shore of Suminoyé in his boat.

Summer days were then as now,—all drowsy and tender blue, with only some light, pure white clouds hanging over the mirror of the sea. Then, too, were the hills the same,—far blue soft shapes melting into the blue sky. And the winds were lazy.

And presently the boy, also lazy, let his boat drift as he fished. It was a queer boat, unpainted and rudderless, of a shape you probably never saw. But still, after fourteen hundred years, there are such boats to be seen in front of the ancient fishing-hamlets of the coast of the Sea of Japan.

After long waiting, Urashima caught something, and drew it up to him. But he found it was only a tortoise.

Now a tortoise is sacred to the Dragon God of the Sea, and the period of its natural life is a thousand—some say ten thousand—years. So that to kill it is very wrong. The boy gently unfastened the creature from his line, and set it free, with a prayer to the gods.

But he caught nothing more. And the day was very warm; and sea and air and all things were very, very silent. And a great drowsiness grew upon him,—and he slept in his drifting boat.

Then out of the dreaming of the sea rose up a beautiful girl,—just as you can see her in the picture to Professor Chamberlain's

"Urashima,"—robed in crimson and blue, with long black hair flowing down her back even to her feet, after the fashion of a prince's daughter fourteen hundred years ago.

Gliding over the waters she came, softly as air; and she stood above the sleeping boy in the boat, and woke him with a light touch, and said:—

"Do not be surprised. My father, the Dragon King of the Sea, sent me to you, because of your kind heart. For to-day you set free a tortoise. And now we will go to my father's palace in the island where summer never dies; and I will be your flower-wife if you wish; and we shall live there happily forever."

And Urashima wondered more and more as he looked upon her; for she was more beautiful than any human being, and he could not but love her. Then she took one oar, and he took another, and they rowed away together,—just as you may still see, off the far western coast, wife and husband rowing together, when the fishing-boats flit into the evening gold.

They rowed away softly and swiftly over the silent blue water down into the south,—till they came to the island where summer never dies,—and to the palace of the Dragon King of the Sea.

(Here the text of the little book suddenly shrinks away as you read, and faint blue ripplings flood the page; and beyond them in a fairy horizon you can see the long low soft shore of the island, and peaked roofs rising through evergreen foliage—the roofs of the Sea God's palace—like the palace of the Mikado Yuriaku, fourteen hundred and sixteen years ago.)

There strange servitors came to receive them in robes of ceremony—creatures of the Sea, who paid greeting to Urashima as the son-in-law of the Dragon King.

So the Sea God's daughter became the bride of Urashima; and it was a bridal festivity of wondrous splendor; and in the Dragon Palace there was great rejoicing.

And each day for Urashima there were new wonders and new pleasures:—wonders of the deepest deep brought up by the servants of the Ocean God;—pleasures of that enchanted land where summer never dies. And so three years passed.

But in spite of all these things, the fisher-boy felt always a heaviness at his heart when he thought of his parents waiting alone. So that at last he prayed his bride to let him go home for a little while only, just to say one word to his father and mother,—after which he would hasten back to her.

At these words she began to weep; and for a long time she continued to weep silently. Then she said to him: "Since you wish to go, of course you must go. I fear your going very much; I fear we shall never see each other again. But I will give you a little box to take with you. It will help you to come back to me if you will do what I tell you. Do not open it. Above all things, do not open it,—no matter what may happen! Because, if you open it, you will never be able to come back, and you will never see me again."

Then she gave him a little lacquered box tied about with a silken cord. (And that box can be seen unto this day in the temple of Kanagawa, by the seashore; and the priests there also keep Urashima Tarō's fishing line, and some strange jewels which he brought back with him from the realm of the Dragon King.)

But Urashima comforted his bride, and promised her never, never to open the box—never even to loosen the silken string. Then he passed away through the summer light over the ever-sleeping sea;—and the shape of the island where summer never dies faded behind him like a dream;—and he saw again before him the blue mountains of Japan, sharpening in the white glow of the northern horizon.

Again at last he glided into his native bay;—again he stood upon its beach. But as he looked, there came upon him a great bewilderment,—a weird doubt.

For the place was at once the same, and yet not the same. The cottage of his fathers had disappeared. There was a village; but the shapes of the houses were all strange, and the trees were strange, and the fields, and even the faces of the people. Nearly all remembered landmarks were gone;—the Shintō temple appeared to have been rebuilt in a new place; the woods had vanished from the neighboring slopes. Only the voice of the little stream flowing through the settlement, and the forms of the mountains, were still the same. All else was unfamiliar and new. In vain he tried to find the dwelling of his parents; and the fisherfolk stared wonderingly at him; and he could not remember having ever seen any of those faces before.

There came along a very old man, leaning on a stick, and Urashima asked him the way to the house of the Urashima family. But the old man looked quite astonished, and made him repeat the question many times, and then cried out:—"Urashima Tarō! Where do you come from that you do not know the story? Urashima Tarō! Why, it is more than four hundred years since he was drowned, and a monument is erected to his memory in the graveyard. The graves of all his people are in that graveyard,—the old graveyard which is not now used any more. Urashima Tarō! How can you be so foolish as to ask where his house is?" And the old man hobbled on, laughing at the simplicity of his questioner.

But Urashima went to the village graveyard,—the old grave-yard that was not used any more,—and there he found his own tombstone, and the tombstones of his father and his mother and his kindred, and the tombstones of many others he had known. So old they were, so moss-eaten, that it was very hard to read the names upon them.

Then he knew himself the victim of some strange illusion, and he took his way back to the beach,—always carrying in his hand the box, the gift of the Sea God's daughter. But what was this illusion? And what could be in that box? Or might not that which was in the box be the cause of the illusion? Doubt mastered faith. Recklessly he broke the promise made to his beloved;—he loosened the silken cord;—he opened the box!

Instantly, without any sound, there burst from it a white cold spectral vapor that rose in air like a summer cloud, and began to drift away swiftly into the south, over the silent sea. There was nothing else in the box.

And Urashima then knew that he had destroyed his own happiness,—that he could never again return to his beloved, the daughter of the Sea King. So that he wept and cried out bitterly in his despair.

Yet for a moment only. In another, he himself was changed. An icy chill shot through all his blood;—his teeth fell out; his face shriveled; his hair turned white as snow; his limbs withered; his strength ebbed; he sank down lifeless on the sand, crushed by the weight of four hundred winters.

Now in the official annals of the Emperors it is written that "in the twenty-first year of the Mikado Yuriaku, the boy Urashima of Midzunoyé, in the district of Yosa, in the province of Tango, a descendant of the divinity Shimanemi, went to Elysium (*Hōrai*) in a fishing-boat." After this there is no more news of Urashima during the reigns of thirty-one emperors and empresses—that is, from the fifth until the ninth century. And then the annals announce that "in the second year of Tenchiyō, in the reign of the Mikado Go-Junwa, the boy Urashima returned, and presently departed again, none knew whither."

III

The fairy mistress came back to tell me that everything was ready, and tried to lift my valise in her slender hands,—which I prevented her from doing, because it was heavy. Then she laughed, but would not suffer that I should carry it myself, and summoned a sea creature with Chinese characters upon his back. I made obeisance to her; and she prayed me to remember the unworthy house despite the rudeness of the maidens. "And you will pay the kurumaya," she said, "only seventy-five sen."

Then I slipped into the vehicle; and in a few minutes the little gray town had vanished behind a curve. I was rolling along a white road overlooking the shore. To the right were pale brown cliffs; to the left only space and sea.

Mile after mile I rolled along that shore, looking into the infinite light. All was steeped in blue,—a marvelous blue, like that which comes and goes in the heart of a great shell. Glowing blue sea met hollow blue sky in a brightness of electric fusion; and vast blue apparitions—the mountains of Higo—angled up through the blaze, like masses of amethyst. What a blue transparency! The universal color was broken only by the dazzling white of a few high summer clouds, motionlessly curled above one phantom peak in the offing. They threw down upon the water snowy tremulous lights. Midges of ships creeping far away seemed to pull long threads after them,—the only sharp lines in all that hazy glory. But what divine clouds! White purified spirits of clouds, resting on their way to the beatitude of Nirvana? Or perhaps the mists escaped from Urashima's box a thousand years ago?

The gnat of the soul of me flitted out into that dream of blue, 'twixt sea and sun,—hummed back to the shore of Suminoyé through the luminous ghosts of fourteen hundred summers. Vaguely I felt beneath me the drifting of a keel. It was the time of the Mikado Yuriaku. And the Daughter of the Dragon King said tinklingly,—"Now we will go to my father's palace where it is always blue." "Why always blue?" I asked. "Because," she said, "I put all the clouds into the Box." "But I must go home," I answered resolutely. "Then," she said, "you will pay the kurumaya only seventy-five sen."

Wherewith I woke into Doyō, or the Period of Greatest Heat, in the twenty-sixth year of Meiji—and saw proof of the era in a line of telegraph poles reaching out of sight on the land side of the way. The kuruma was still fleeing by the shore, before the same blue vision of sky, peak, and sea; but the white clouds were gone!—and there were no more cliffs close to the road, but fields of rice and of barley stretching to far-off hills. The telegraph lines absorbed my attention for a moment, because on the top wire, and only on the top wire, hosts of little birds were perched, all with their heads to the road, and nowise disturbed by our coming. They remained quite still, looking down upon us as mere passing phenomena. There were hundreds and hundreds in rank, for miles and miles. And I could not see one having its tail turned to the road. Why they sat thus, and what they were watching or waiting for, I could not guess. At intervals I waved my hat and shouted, to startle the ranks. Whereupon a few would rise up fluttering and chippering, and drop back again upon the wire in the same position as before. The vast majority refused to take me seriously.

The sharp rattle of the wheels was drowned by a deep booming; and as we whirled past a village I caught sight of an immense drum under an open shed, beaten by naked men.

"O kurumaya!" I shouted—"that—what is it?"

He, without stopping, shouted back:—

"Everywhere now the same thing is. Much time-in rain has not been: so the gods to prayers are made, and drums are beaten."

We flashed through other villages; and I saw and heard more drums of various sizes, and from hamlets invisible, over miles of parching rice-fields, yet other drums, like echoings, responded.

IV

Then I began to think about Urashima again. I thought of the pictures and poems and proverbs recording the influence of the legend upon the imagination of a race. I thought of an Izumo dancing-girl I saw at a banquet acting the part of Urashima, with a little lacquered box whence there issued at the tragical minute a mist of Kyōto incense. I thought about the antiquity of the beautiful dance,—and therefore about vanished generations of dancing-girls,—and therefore about dust in the abstract; which, again, led me to think of dust in the concrete, as bestirred by the sandals of the kurumaya to whom I was to pay only seventy-five sen. And I wondered how much of it might be old human dust, and whether in the eternal order of things the motion of hearts might be of more consequence than the motion of dust. Then my ancestral morality took alarm; and I tried to persuade myself that a story which had lived for a thousand years, gaining fresher charm with the passing of every century, could only have survived by virtue of some truth in it. But what truth? For the time being I could find no answer to this question.

The heat had become very great; and I cried,—

"O kurumaya! the throat of Selfishness is dry; water desirable is."

He, still running, answered:—

"The Village of the Long Beach inside of—not far—a great gush-water is. There pure august water will be given."

I cried again:—

"O kurumaya!—those little birds as-for, why this way always facing?"

He, running still more swiftly, responded:—

"All birds wind-to facing sit."

I laughed first at my own simplicity; then at my forgetfulness,— remembering I had been told the same thing, somewhere or other, when a boy. Perhaps the mystery of Urashima might also have been created by forgetfulness.

I thought again about Urashima. I saw the Daughter of the Dragon King waiting vainly in the palace made beautiful for his welcome,—and the pitiless return of the Cloud, announcing what had happened,—and the loving uncouth sea-creatures, in their garments of great ceremony, trying to comfort her. But in the real story there was nothing of all this; and the pity of the people seemed to be all for Urashima. And I began to discourse with myself thus:—

Is it right to pity Urashima at all? Of course he was bewildered by the gods. But who is not bewildered by the gods? What is Life itself but a bewilderment? And Urashima in his bewilderment doubted the purpose of the gods, and opened the box. Then he died without any trouble, and the people built a shrine to him as Urashima Miō-jin. Why, then, so much pity?

Things are quite differently managed in the West. After disobeying Western gods, we have still to remain alive and to learn the height and the breadth and the depth of superlative sorrow. We are not allowed to die quite comfortably just at the best possible time: much less are we suffered to become after death small gods in our own right. How can we pity the folly of Urashima after he had lived so long alone with visible gods?

Perhaps the fact that we do may answer the riddle. This pity must be self-pity; wherefore the legend may be the legend of a myriad souls. The thought of it comes just at a particular time of blue light and soft wind,—and always like an old reproach. It has too intimate relation to a season and the feeling of a season not to be also related to something real in one's life, or in the lives of one's ancestors. But what was that real something? Who was the Daughter of the Dragon King? Where was the island of unending summer? And what was the cloud in the box?

I cannot answer all those questions. I know this only,—which is not at all new:—

I have memory of a place and a magical time in which the Sun and the Moon were larger and brighter than now. Whether it was of this life or of some life before I cannot tell. But I know the sky was very much more blue, and nearer to the world,—almost as it seems to become above the masts of a steamer steaming into equatorial summer. The sea was alive, and used to talk,—and the Wind made me cry out for joy when it touched me. Once or twice during other years, in divine days lived among the peaks, I have dreamed just for a moment that the same wind was blowing,—but it was only a remembrance.

Also in that place the clouds were wonderful, and of colors for which there are no names at all,—colors that used to make me hungry and thirsty. I remember, too, that the days were ever so much longer than these days,—and that every day there were new wonders and new pleasures for me. And all that country and time were softly ruled by One who thought only of ways to make me happy. Sometimes I would refuse to be made happy, and that always caused her pain, although she was divine;—and I remember that I tried very hard to be sorry. When day was done, and there fell the great hush of the light before moonrise, she would tell me stories that made me tingle from head to foot with pleasure. I have never heard any other stories half so beautiful. And when the pleasure became too great, she would sing a weird little song which always brought sleep. At last there came a parting day; and she wept, and told me of a charm she had given that I must never, never lose, because it would keep me young, and give me power to return. But I never returned. And the years went; and one day I knew that I had lost the charm, and had become ridiculously old.

The Village of the Long Beach is at the foot of a green cliff near the road, and consists of a dozen thatched cottages clustered about a rocky pool, shaded by pines. The basin overflows with cold water, supplied by a stream that leaps straight from the heart of the cliff,—just as folks imagine that a poem ought to spring straight from the heart of a poet. It was evidently a favorite halting-place, judging by the number of kuruma and of people resting. There were benches under the trees; and, after having allayed thirst, I sat down to smoke and to look at the women washing clothes and the travelers refreshing themselves at the pool,—while my kurumaya stripped, and proceeded to dash buckets of cold water over his body. Then tea was brought me by a young man with a baby on his back; and I tried to play with the baby, which said "Ah, bah!"

Such are the first sounds uttered by a Japanese babe. But they are purely Oriental; and in Komaji should be written *Aba*. And, as an utterance untaught, *Aba* is interesting.

It is in Japanese child-speech the word for "good-bye,"—precisely the last we would expect an infant to pronounce on entering into this world of illusion. To whom or to what is the little soul saying good-bye?—to friends in a previous state of existence still freshly remembered?—to comrades of its shadowy journey from nobody-knows-where? Such theorizing is tolerably safe, from a pious point of view, since the child can never decide for us. What its thoughts were at that mysterious moment of first speech, it will have forgotten long before it has become able to answer questions.

Unexpectedly, a queer recollection came to me,—resurrected, perhaps, by the sight of the young man with the baby,—perhaps by the song of the water in the cliff: the recollection of a story:—

Long, long ago there lived somewhere among the mountains a poor wood-cutter and his wife. They were very old, and had no children. Every day the husband went alone to the forest to cut wood, while the wife sat weaving at home.

One day the old man went farther into the forest than was his custom, to seek a certain kind of wood; and he suddenly found himself at the edge of a little spring he had never seen before. The water was strangely clear and cold, and he was thirsty; for the day was hot, and he had been working hard. So he doffed his great straw hat, knelt down, and took a long drink. That water seemed to refresh him in a most extraordinary way. Then he caught sight of his own face in the spring, and started back. It was certainly his own face, but not at all as he was accustomed to see it in the old mirror at home. It was the face of a very young man! He could not believe his eyes. He put up both hands to his head, which had been quite bald only a moment before. It was covered with thick black hair. And his face had become smooth as a boy's; every wrinkle was gone. At the same moment he discovered himself full of new strength. He stared in astonishment at the limbs that had been so long withered by age; they were now shapely and hard with dense young muscle. Unknowingly he had drunk at the Fountain of Youth; and that draught had transformed him.

First, he leaped high and shouted for joy; then he ran home faster than he had ever run before in his life. When he entered his house his wife was frightened,—because she took him for a stranger; and when he told her the wonder, she could not at once believe him. But after a long time he was able to convince her that the young man she now saw before her was really her husband; and he told her where the spring was, and asked her to go there with him.

Then she said: "You have become so handsome and so young that you cannot continue to love an old woman;—so I must drink some of that water immediately. But it will never do for both of us to be away from the house at the same time. Do you wait here while I go." And she ran to the woods all by herself.

She found the spring and knelt down, and began to drink. Oh! how cool and sweet that water was ! She drank and drank and drank, and stopped for breath only to begin again.

Her husband waited for her impatiently; he expected to see her come back changed into a pretty slender girl. But she did not come back at all. He got anxious, shut up the house, and went to look for her.

When he reached the spring, he could not see her. He was just on the point of returning when he heard a little wail in the high grass near the spring. He searched there and discovered his wife's clothes and a baby,—a very small baby, perhaps six months old!

For the old woman had drunk too deeply of the magical water; she had drunk herself far back beyond the time of youth into the period of speechless infancy.

He took up the child in his arms. It looked at him in a sad, wondering way. He carried it home,—murmuring to it,—thinking strange, melancholy thoughts.

In that hour, after my reverie about Urashima, the moral of this story seemed less satisfactory than in former time. Because by drinking too deeply of life we do not become young.

Naked and cool my kurumaya returned, and said that because of the heat he could not finish the promised run of twenty-five miles, but that he had found another runner to take me the rest of the way. For so much as he himself had done, he wanted fifty-five sen.

It was really very hot—more than 100 degrees I afterwards learned; and far away there throbbed continually, like a pulsation of the heat itself, the sound of great drums beating for rain. And I thought of the Daughter of the Dragon King. "Seventy-five sen, she told me," I observed;—"and that promised to be done has not been done. Nevertheless, seventy-five sen to you shall be given,—because I am afraid of the gods."

And behind a yet unwearied runner I fled away into the enormous blaze—in the direction of the great drums.

■ A Legend of Fugen-Bosatsu

There was once a very pious and learned priest, called Shōku Shōnin, who lived in the province of Harima. For many years he meditated daily upon the chapter of Fugen-Bosatsu (the Bodhisattva Samantabhadra) in the Sûtra of the Lotos of the Good Law; and he used to pray, every morning and evening, that he might at some time be permitted to behold Fugen-Bosatsu as a living presence, and in the form described in the holy text.[*]

One evening, while he was reciting the Sûtra, drowsiness overcame him; and he fell asleep leaning upon his *kyōsoku*.[†] Then he dreamed; and in his dream a voice told him that, in order to see Fugen-Bosatsu, he must go to the house of a certain courtesan,

---

[*] The priest's desire was probably inspired by the promises recorded in the chapter titled "The Encouragement of Samantabhadra" of *The Lotus Sutra*—"Then the Bodhisattva Mahâsattva Samantabhadra said to the Lord: . . . 'When a preacher who applies himself to this Dharmaparyâya shall take a walk, then, O Lord, will I mount a white elephant with six tusks, and betake myself to the place where that preacher is walking, in order to protect this Dharmaparyâya. And when that preacher, applying himself to this Dharmaparyâya, forgets, be it but a single word or syllable, then I will mount the white elephant with six tusks, and show my face to that preacher, and repeat this entire Dharmaparyâya.'"—But these promises refer to "the end of time."

[†] The *kyōsoku* is a kind of padded arm-rest, or arm-stool, upon which the priest leans one arm while reading. The use of such an arm-rest is not confined, however, to the Buddhist clergy.

known as the "Yujō-no-Chōja,"* who lived in the town of Kanzaki. Immediately upon awakening he resolved to go to Kanzaki;—and, making all possible haste, he reached the town by the evening of the next day.

When he entered the house of the *yujō*, he found many persons already there assembled—mostly young men of the capital, who had been attracted to Kanzaki by the fame of the woman's beauty. They were feasting and drinking; and the *yujō* was playing a small hand-drum (*tsuzumi*), which she used very skillfully, and singing a song. The song which she sang was an old Japanese song about a famous shrine in the town of Murozumi; and the words were these:—

> Within the sacred water-tank† of Murozumi in Suwō,
> Even though no wind be blowing,
> The surface of the water is always rippling.

The sweetness of the voice filled everybody with surprise and delight. As the priest, who had taken a place apart, listened and wondered, the girl suddenly fixed her eyes upon him; and in the same instant he saw her form change into the form of Fugen-Bosatsu, emitting from her brow a beam of light that seemed to pierce beyond the limits of the universe, and riding a snow-white elephant with six tusks. And still she sang—but the song also

---

* A *yujō*, in old days, was a singing-girl as well as a courtesan. The term "Yujō-no-Chōja," in this case, would mean simply "the first (or best) of yujō."

† *Mitarai, Mitarai* (or *mitarashi*) is the name especially given to the water-tanks, or the water-fonts—of stone or bronze—placed before Shintō shrines in order that the worshipper may purify his lips and hands before making prayer. Buddhist tanks are not so named.

was now transformed; and the words came thus to the ears of the priest:—

> On the Vast Sea of Cessation,
> Though the Winds of the Six Desires and of the Five
> Corruptions never blow,
> Yet the surface of that deep is always covered
> With the billowings of Attainment to the Reality-in-Itself.

Dazzled by the divine ray, the priest closed his eyes: but through their lids he still distinctly saw the vision. When he opened them again, it was gone: he saw only the girl with her hand-drum, and heard only the song about the water of Murozumi. But he found that as often as he shut his eyes he could see Fugen-Bosatsu on the six-tusked elephant, and could hear the mystic Song of the Sea of Cessation. The other persons present saw only the *yujō*: they had not beheld the manifestation.

Then the singer suddenly disappeared from the banquet-room—none could say when or how. From that moment the revelry ceased; and gloom took the place of joy. After having waited and sought for the girl to no purpose, the company dispersed in great sorrow. Last of all, the priest departed, bewildered by the emotions of the evening. But scarcely had he passed beyond the gate, when the *yujō* appeared before him, and said:—"Friend, do not speak yet to any one of what you have seen this night." And with these words she vanished away,—leaving the air filled with a delicious fragrance.

The monk by whom the foregoing legend was recorded, comments upon it thus:—The condition of a *yujō* is low and miserable, since she is condemned to serve the lusts of men. Who therefore could imagine that such a woman might be the *nirmanakaya,* or incarnation, of a Bodhisattva. But we must remember that the Buddhas and the Bodhisattvas may appear in this world in countless different forms; choosing, for the purpose of their divine compassion, even the most humble or contemptible shapes when such shapes can serve them to lead men into the true path, and to save them from the perils of illusion.

Says the old Japanese author, Hakubai-En Rosui:—*

"In Chinese and in Japanese books there are related many stories,—both of ancient and of modern times,—about pictures that were so beautiful as to exercise a magical influence upon the beholder. And concerning such beautiful pictures,—whether pictures of flowers or of birds or of people, painted by famous artists,—it is further told that the shapes of the creatures or the persons, therein depicted, would separate themselves from the paper or the silk upon which they had been painted, and would perform various acts;—so that they became, by their own will, really alive. We shall not now repeat any of the stories of this class which have been known to everybody from ancient times. But even in modern times the fame of the pictures painted by Hishigawa Kichibei—'Hishigawa's Portraits'—has become widespread in the land."

He then proceeds to relate the following story about one of the so-called portraits:—

* He died in the eighteenth year of Kyōhō (1733). The painter to whom he refers— better known to collectors as Hishigawa Kichibei Moronobu—flourished during the latter part of the seventeenth century. Beginning his career as a dyer's apprentice, he won his reputation as an artist about 1680, when he may be said to have founded the Ukiyo-yé school of illustration. Hishigawa was especially a delineator of what are called *fūryū* ("elegant manners"),—the aspects of life among the upper classes of society.

There was a young scholar of Kyōto whose name was Tokkei. He used to live in the street called Muromachi. One evening, while on his way home after a visit, his attention was attracted by an old single-leaf screen (*tsuitaté*), exposed for sale before the shop of a dealer in second-hand goods. It was only a paper-covered screen; but there was painted upon it the full-length figure of a girl which caught the young man's fancy. The price asked was very small: Tokkei bought the screen, and took it home with him.

When he looked again at the screen, in the solitude of his own room, the picture seemed to him much more beautiful than before. Apparently it was a real likeness,—the portrait of a girl fifteen or sixteen years old; and every little detail in the painting of the hair, eyes, eyelashes, mouth, had been executed with a delicacy and a truth beyond praise. The *manajiri*[*] seemed "like a lotus-blossom courting favor"; the lips were "like the smile of a red flower"; the whole young face was inexpressibly sweet. If the real girl so portrayed had been equally lovely, no man could have looked upon her without losing his heart. And Tokkei believed that she must have been thus lovely;—for the figure seemed alive,—ready to reply to anybody who might speak to it.

Gradually, as he continued to gaze at the picture, he felt himself bewitched by the charm of it. "Can there really have been in this world," he murmured to himself, "so delicious a creature? How gladly would I give my life—nay, a thousand years of life!—to hold her in my arms even for a moment!" (The Japanese author says "for a few seconds.") In short, he became enamored of the picture,—so

---

[*] Also written *méjiri*,—the exterior canthus of the eye. The Japanese (like the old Greek and the old Arabian poets) have many curious dainty words and similes to express particular beauties of the hair, eyes, eyelids, lips, fingers, etc.

much enamored of it as to feel that he never could love any woman except the person whom it represented. Yet that person, if still alive, could no longer resemble the painting: perhaps she had been buried long before he was born!

Day by day, nevertheless, this hopeless passion grew upon him. He could not eat; he could not sleep: neither could he occupy his mind with those studies which had formerly delighted him. He would sit for hours before the picture, talking to it,—neglecting or forgetting everything else. And at last he fell sick—so sick that he believed himself going to die.

Now among the friends of Tokkei there was one venerable scholar who knew many strange things about old pictures and about young hearts. This aged scholar, hearing of Tokkei's illness, came to visit him, and saw the screen, and understood what had happened. Then Tokkei, being questioned, confessed everything to his friend, and declared:—"If I cannot find such a woman, I shall die."

The old man said:—

"That picture was painted by Hishigawa Kichibei,—painted from life. The person whom it represented is not now in the world. But it is said that Hishigawa Kichibei painted her mind as well as her form, and that her spirit lives in the picture. So I think that you can win her."

Tokkei half rose from his bed, and stared eagerly at the speaker.

"You must give her a name," the old man continued;—"and you must sit before her picture every day, and keep your thoughts constantly fixed upon her, and call her gently by the name which you have given her, *until she answers you. . . .*"

"Answers me!" exclaimed the lover, in breathless amazement.

"Oh, yes," the adviser responded, "she will certainly answer you. But you must be ready, when she answers you, to present her with what I am going to tell you. . . ."

"I will give her my life!" cried Tokkei.

"No," said the old man;—"you will present her with a cup of wine that has been bought at one hundred different wine-shops. Then she will come out of the screen to accept the wine. After that, probably she herself will tell you what to do."

With these words the old man went away. His advice aroused Tokkei from despair. At once he seated himself before the picture, and called it by the name of a girl (what name the Japanese narrator has forgotten to tell us) over and over again, very tenderly. That day it made no answer, nor the next day, nor the next. But Tokkei did not lose faith or patience; and after many days it suddenly one evening answered to its name,—

"*Hai!*" (Yes.)

Then quickly, quickly, some of the wine from a hundred different wine-shops was poured out, and reverentially presented in a little cup. And the girl stepped from the screen, and walked upon the matting of the room, and knelt to take the cup from Tokkei's hand,—asking, with a delicious smile:—

"How could you love me so much?"

Says the Japanese narrator: "She was much more beautiful than the picture,—beautiful to the tips of her finger-nails,—beautiful also in heart and temper,—lovelier than anybody else in the world." What answer Tokkei made to her question is not recorded: it will have to be imagined.

"But will you not soon get tired of me?" she asked.

"Never while I live!" he protested.

"And after—?" she persisted;—for the Japanese bride is not satisfied with love for one life-time only.

"Let us pledge ourselves to each other," he entreated, "for the time of seven existences."

"If you are ever unkind to me," she said, "I will go back to the screen."

They pledged each other. I suppose that Tokkei was a good boy,—for his bride never returned to the screen. The space that she had occupied upon it remained a blank.

Exclaims the Japanese author,—

"How very seldom do such things happen in this world!"

The body was cold as ice; the heart had long ceased to beat: yet there were no other signs of death. Nobody even spoke of burying the woman. She had died of grief and anger at having been divorced. It would have been useless to bury her,—because the last undying wish of a dying person for vengeance can burst asunder any tomb and rift the heaviest graveyard stone. People who lived near the house in which she was lying fled from their homes. They knew that she was only *waiting for the return of the man who had divorced her.*

At the time of her death he was on a journey. When he came back and was told what had happened, terror seized him. "If I can find no help before dark," he thought to himself, "she will tear me to pieces." It was yet only the Hour of the Dragon;* but he knew that he had no time to lose.

He went at once to an *inyōshi*† and begged for succor. The *inyōshi* knew the story of the dead woman; and he had seen the body. He said to the supplicant:—"A very great danger threatens you. I will try to save you. But you must promise to do whatever I shall tell

* *Tasu no Koku,* or the Hour of the Dragon, by old Japanese time, began at about eight o'clock in the morning.

† *Inyōshi,* a professor or master of the science of *in-yō,*—the old Chinese nature-philosophy, based upon the theory of a male and a female principle pervading the universe.

you to do. There is only one way by which you can be saved. It is a fearful way. But unless you find the courage to attempt it, she will tear you limb from limb. If you can be brave, come to me again in the evening before sunset." The man shuddered; but he promised to do whatever should be required of him.

At sunset the *inyōshi* went with him to the house where the body was lying. The *inyōshi* pushed open the sliding-doors, and told his client to enter. It was rapidly growing dark. "I dare not!" gasped the man, quaking from head to foot;—"I dare not even look at her!" "You will have to do much more than look at her," declared the *inyōshi*;—"and you promised to obey. Go in!" He forced the trembler into the house and led him to the side of the corpse.

The dead woman was lying on her face. "Now you must get astride upon her," said the *inyōshi*, "and sit firmly on her back, as if you were riding a horse. . . . Come!—you must do it!" The man shivered so that the *inyōshi* had to support him—shivered horribly; but he obeyed. "Now take her hair in your hands," commanded the *inyōshi*,—"half in the right hand, half in the left. . . . So! . . . You must grip it like a bridle. Twist your hands in it—both hands— tightly. That is the way! . . . Listen to me! You must stay like that till morning. You will have reason to be afraid in the night—plenty of reason. But whatever may happen, never let go of her hair. If you let go,—even for one second,—she will tear you into gobbets!"

The *inyōshi* then whispered some mysterious words into the ear of the body, and said to its rider:—"Now, for my own sake, I must leave you alone with her. . . . Remain as you are! . . . Above all things, remember that you must not let go of her hair." And he went away,—closing the doors behind him.

Hour after hour the man sat upon the corpse in black fear;— and the hush of the night deepened and deepened about him till he screamed to break it. Instantly the body sprang beneath him, as to cast him off; and the dead woman cried out loudly, "Oh, how heavy it is! Yet I shall bring that fellow here now!"

Then tall she rose, and leaped to the doors, and flung them open, and rushed into the night,—always bearing the weight of the man. But he, shutting his eyes, kept his hands twisted in her long hair,— tightly, tightly,—though fearing with such a fear that he could not even moan. How far she went, he never knew. He saw nothing: he heard only the sound of her naked feet in the dark,—*picha-picha, picha-picha*,—and the hiss of her breathing as she ran.

At last she turned, and ran back into the house, and lay down upon the floor exactly as at first. Under the man she panted and moaned till the cocks began to crow. Thereafter she lay still.

But the man, with chattering teeth, sat upon her until the *inyōshi* came at sunrise. "So you did not let go of her hair!"—observed the *inyōshi*, greatly pleased. "That is well. . . . Now you can stand up." He whispered again into the ear of the corpse, and then said to the man:—"You must have passed a fearful night; but nothing else could have saved you. Hereafter you may feel secure from her vengeance."

In Kyōto there is a famous temple called Amadera. Sadazumi Shinnō, the fifth son of the Emperor Seiwa, passed the greater part of his life there as a priest; and the graves of many celebrated persons are to be seen in the temple-grounds.

But the present edifice is not the ancient Amadera. The original temple, after the lapse of ten centuries, fell into such decay that it had to be entirely rebuilt in the fourteenth year of Genroku (1701 A.D.).

A great festival was held to celebrate the rebuilding of the Amadera; and among the thousands of persons who attended that festival there was a young scholar and poet named Hanagaki Baishū. He wandered about the newly laid-out grounds and gardens, delighted by all that he saw, until he reached the place of a spring at which he had often drunk in former times. He was then surprised to find that the soil about the spring had been dug away, so as to form a square pond, and that at one corner of this pond there had been set up a wooden tablet bearing the words *Tanjō-Sui* ("Birth-Water").* He also saw that a small, but very handsome temple of the Goddess Benten had been erected beside the pond. While he

---

* The word *tanjō* (birth) should here be understood in its mystical Buddhist meaning of new life or rebirth, rather than in the Western signification of birth.

was looking at this new temple, a sudden gust of wind blew to his feet a *tanzaku*,* on which the following poem had been written:—

Shirushi aréto
Iwai zo somuru
Tama hōki,
Toruté bakari no
Chigiri narétomo.

This poem—a poem on first love (*hatsu koi*), composed by the famous Shunrei Kyō—was not unfamiliar to him; but it had been written upon the *tanzaku* by a female hand, and so exquisitely that he could scarcely believe his eyes. Something in the form of the characters,—an indefinite grace,—suggested that period of youth between childhood and womanhood; and the pure rich color of the ink seemed to bespeak the purity and goodness of the writer's heart.†

Baishū carefully folded up the *tanzaku*, and took it home with him. When he looked at it again the writing appeared to him even more wonderful than at first. His knowledge in calligraphy assured him only that the poem had been written by some girl who was

---

* *Tanzaku* is the name given to the long strips or ribbons of paper that are suspended from trees in flower, from wind-bells, from any beautiful object in which the poet has found an inspiration.

† It is difficult for the inexperienced European eye to distinguish in Chinese or Japanese writing those characteristics implied by our term "hand"—in the sense of individual style. But the Japanese scholar never forgets the peculiarities of a handwriting once seen; and he can even guess at the approximate age of the writer. Chinese and Japanese authors claim that the color (quality) of the ink used tells something of the character of the writer. As every person grounds or prepares his or her own ink, the deeper and clearer black would at least indicate something of personal carefulness and of the sense of beauty.

very young, very intelligent, and probably very gentle-hearted. But this assurance sufficed to shape within his mind the image of a very charming person; and he soon found himself in love with the unknown. Then his first resolve was to seek out the writer of the verses, and, if possible, make her his wife. . . . Yet how was he to find her? Who was she? Where did she live? Certainly he could hope to find her only through the favor of the Gods.

But presently it occurred to him that the Gods might be very willing to lend their aid. The *tanzaku* had come to him while he was standing in front of the temple of Benten-Sama; and it was to this divinity in particular that lovers were wont to pray for happy union. This reflection impelled him to beseech the Goddess for assistance. He went at once to the temple of Benten-of-the-Birth-Water (*Tanjō-sui-no-Benten*) in the grounds of the Amadera; and there, with all the fervor of his heart, he made his petition:—"O Goddess, pity me!—help me to find where the young person lives who wrote the *tanzaku*!—vouchsafe me but one chance to meet her,—even if only for a moment!" And after having made this prayer, he began to perform a seven days' religious service (*nanuka-mairi*)* in honor of the Goddess; vowing at the same time to pass the seventh night in ceaseless worship before her shrine.

Now on the seventh night,—the night of his vigil,—during the hour when the silence is most deep, he heard at the main gateway of the temple-grounds a voice calling for admittance. Another voice from within answered; the gate was opened; and Baishū saw an old man of majestic appearance approaching with slow steps. This venerable person was clad in robes of ceremony; and he wore upon his

* There are many kinds of religious exercises called *mairi*. The performer of a *nanuka-mairi* pledges himself to pray at a certain temple every day for seven days in succession.

snow-white head a black cap (*eboshi*) of the form indicating high rank. Reaching the little temple of Benten, he knelt down in front of it, as if respectfully awaiting some order. Then the outer door of the temple was opened; the hanging curtain of bamboo behind it, concealing the inner sanctuary, was rolled half-way up; and a *chigo*[*] came forward,—a beautiful boy, with long hair tied back in the ancient manner. He stood at the threshold, and said to the old man in a clear loud voice:—

"There is a person here who has been praying for a love-union not suitable to his present condition, and otherwise difficult to bring about. But as the young man is worthy of Our pity, you have been called to see whether something can be done for him. If there should prove to be any relation between the parties from the period of a former birth, you will introduce them to each other."

On receiving this command, the old man bowed respectfully to the *chigo*: then, rising, he drew from the pocket of his long left sleeve a crimson cord. One end of this cord he passed round Baishū's body, as if to bind him with it. The other end he put into the flame of one of the temple-lamps; and while the cord was there burning, he waved his hand three times, as if to summon somebody out of the dark.

Immediately, in the direction of the Amadera, a sound of coming steps was heard; and in another moment a girl appeared,—a charming girl, fifteen or sixteen years old. She approached gracefully, but very shyly,—hiding the lower part of her face with a fan; and she knelt down beside Baishū. The *chigo* then said to Baishū:—

[*] The term *chigo* usually means the page of a noble household, especially an imperial page. The *chigo* who appears in this story is of course a supernatural being,—the court-messenger of the Goddess, and her mouthpiece.

"Recently you have been suffering much heart-pain; and this desperate love of yours has even impaired your health. We could not allow you to remain in so unhappy a condition; and We therefore summoned the Old-Man-under-the-Moon* to make you acquainted with the writer of that *tanzaku*. She is now beside you."

With these words, the *chigo* retired behind the bamboo curtain. Then the old man went away as he had come; and the young girl followed him. Simultaneously Baishū heard the great bell of the Amadera sounding the hour of dawn. He prostrated himself in thanksgiving before the shrine of Benten-of-the-Birth-Water, and proceeded homeward,—feeling as if awakened from some delightful dream,—happy at having seen the charming person whom he had so fervently prayed to meet,—unhappy also because of the fear that he might never meet her again.

But scarcely had he passed from the gateway into the street, when he saw a young girl walking alone in the same direction that he was going; and, even in the dusk of the dawn, he recognized her at once as the person to whom he had been introduced before the temple of Benten. As he quickened his pace to overtake her, she turned and saluted him with a graceful bow. Then for the first time he ventured to speak to her; and she answered him in a voice of which the sweetness filled his heart with joy. Through the yet silent streets they walked on, chatting happily, till they found themselves before the house where Baishū lived. There he paused—spoke to the girl of his hopes and fears. Smiling, she asked:—"Do you not know that I was sent for to become your wife?" And she entered with him.

---

* *Gekkawō.* This is a poetical appellation for the God of Marriage, more usually known as *Musubi-no-kami.* Throughout this story there is an interesting mingling of Shintō and Buddhist ideas.

Becoming his wife, she delighted him beyond expectation by the charm of her mind and heart. Moreover, he found her to be much more accomplished than he had supposed. Besides being able to write so wonderfully, she could paint beautiful pictures; she knew the art of arranging flowers, the art of embroidery, the art of music; she could weave and sew; and she knew everything in regard to the management of a house.

It was in the early autumn that the young people had met; and they lived together in perfect accord until the winter season began. Nothing, during those months, occurred to disturb their peace. Baishū's love for his gentle wife only strengthened with the passing of time. Yet, strangely enough, he remained ignorant of her history,—knew nothing about her family. Of such matters she had never spoken; and, as the Gods had given her to him, he imagined that it would not be proper to question her. But neither the Old-Man-under-the-Moon nor anyone else came—as he had feared—to take her away. Nobody even made any inquiries about her. And the neighbors, for some undiscoverable reason, acted as if totally unaware of her presence.

Baishū wondered at all this. But stranger experiences were awaiting him.

One winter morning he happened to be passing through a somewhat remote quarter of the city, when he heard himself loudly called by name, and saw a man-servant making signs to him from the gateway of a private residence. As Baishū did not know the man's face, and did not have a single acquaintance in that part of Kyōto, he was more than startled by so abrupt a summons. But the servant, coming forward, saluted him with the utmost respect, and said, "My master greatly desires the honor of speaking with you: deign to enter for a moment." After an instant of hesitation, Baishū allowed himself to be conducted to the house. A dignified and richly dressed person, who seemed to be the master, welcomed him at the entrance, and led him to the guest-room. When the courtesies due upon a first meeting had been fully exchanged, the host apologized for the informal manner of his invitation, and said:—

"It must have seemed to you very rude of us to call you in such a way. But perhaps you will pardon our impoliteness when I tell you that we acted thus upon what I firmly believe to have been an inspiration from the Goddess Benten. Now permit me to explain.

"I have a daughter, about sixteen years old, who can write rather well,* and do other things in the common way: she has the ordinary nature of woman. As we were anxious to make her happy by finding a good husband for her, we prayed to the Goddess Benten to help us; and we sent to every temple of Benten in the city a *tanzaku* written by the girl. Some nights later, the Goddess appeared to me in a dream, and said: 'We have heard your prayer, and have already introduced your daughter to the person who is to become her husband. During the coming winter he will visit you.' As I did not understand this assurance that a presentation had been made, I felt some doubt; I thought that the dream might have been only a common dream, signifying nothing. But last night again I saw Benten-Sama in a dream; and she said to me: 'Tomorrow the young man, of whom I once spoke to you, will come to this street: then you

---

* As it is the old Japanese rule that parents should speak depreciatingly of their children's accomplishments, the phrase "rather well" in this connection would mean, for the visitor, "wonderfully well." For the same reason, the expressions "common way" and "ordinary nature," as subsequently used, would imply almost the reverse of the literal meaning.

can call him into your house, and ask him to become the husband of your daughter. He is a good young man; and later in life he will obtain a much higher rank than he now holds.' Then Benten-Sama told me your name, your age, your birthplace, and described your features and dress so exactly that my servant found no difficulty in recognizing you by the indications which I was able to give him."

This explanation bewildered Baishū instead of reassuring him; and his only reply was a formal return of thanks for the honor which the master of the house had spoken of doing him. But when the host invited him to another room, for the purpose of presenting him to the young lady, his embarrassment became extreme. Yet he could not reasonably decline the introduction. He could not bring himself, under such extraordinary circumstances, to announce that he already had a wife,—a wife given to him by the Goddess Benten herself; a wife from whom he could not even think of separating. So, in silence and trepidation, he followed his host to the apartment indicated.

Then what was his amazement to discover, when presented to the daughter of the house, that she was the very same person whom he had already taken to wife!

The same,—yet not the same.

She to whom he had been introduced by the Old-Man-under-the-Moon, was only the soul of the beloved.

She to whom he was now to be wedded, in her father's house, was the body.

Benten had wrought this miracle for the sake of her worshippers.

The original story breaks off suddenly at this point, leaving several matters unexplained. The ending is rather unsatisfactory.

One would like to know something about the mental experiences of the real maiden during the married life of her phantom. One would also like to know what became of the phantom,—whether it continued to lead an independent existence; whether it waited patiently for the return of its husband; whether it paid a visit to the real bride. And the book says nothing about these things. But a Japanese friend explains the miracle thus:—

"The spirit-bride was really formed out of the *tanzaku*. So it is possible that the real girl did not know anything about the meeting at the temple of Benten. When she wrote those beautiful characters upon the *tanzaku*, something of her spirit passed into them. Therefore it was possible to evoke from the writing the double of the writer."

■ The Gratitude of the Samébito

There was a man named Tawaraya Tōtarō, who lived in the Province of Ōmi. His house was situated on the shore of Lake Biwa, not far from the famous temple called Ishiyamadera. He had some property, and lived in comfort; but at the age of twenty-nine he was still unmarried. His greatest ambition was to marry a very beautiful woman; and he had not been able to find a girl to his liking.

One day, as he was passing over the Long Bridge of Séta,* he saw a strange being crouching close to the parapet. The body of this being resembled the body of a man, but was black as ink; its face was like the face of a demon; its eyes were green as emeralds; and its beard was like the beard of a dragon. Tōtarō was at first very much startled. But the green eyes looked at him so gently that after a moment's hesitation he ventured to question the creature. Then it answered him, saying: "I am a *Samébito*,†—a Shark-Man of the

---

* The Long Bridge of Séta (*Séta-no-Naga-Hashi*), famous in Japanese legend, is nearly eight hundred feet in length, and commands a beautiful view. This bridge crosses the waters of the Sétagawa near the junction of the stream with Lake Biwa. Ishiyamadera, one of the most picturesque Buddhist temples in Japan, is situated within a short distance from the bridge.

† Literally, "a Shark-Person," but in this story the *Samébito* is a male. The characters for *Samébito* can also be read *Kōjin*,—which is the usual reading. In dictionaries the word is loosely rendered by "merman" or "mermaid"; but as the preceding description shows, the *Samébito* or *Kōjin* of the Far East is a conception having little in common with the Western idea of a merman or mermaid.

sea; and until a short time ago I was in the service of the Eight Great Dragon-Kings (*Hachi-Dai-Ryū-Ō*) as a subordinate officer in the Dragon-Palace (*Ryūgū*).* But because of a small fault which I committed, I was dismissed from the Dragon-Palace, and also banished from the Sea. Since then I have been wandering about here,—unable to get any food, or even a place to lie down. If you can feel any pity for me, do, I beseech you, help me to find a shelter, and let me have something to eat!"

This petition was uttered in so plaintive a tone, and in so humble a manner, that Tōtarō's heart was touched. "Come with me," he said. "There is in my garden a large and deep pond where you may live as long as you wish; and I will give you plenty to eat."

The Samébito followed Tōtarō home, and appeared to be much pleased with the pond.

Thereafter, for nearly half a year, this strange guest dwelt in the pond, and was every day supplied by Tōtarō with such food as sea-creatures like.

(From this point of the original narrative, the Shark-Man is referred to not as a monster, but as a sympathetic person of the male sex.)

Now, in the seventh month of the same year, there was a female pilgrimage (*nyonin-mōdé*) to the great Buddhist temple called Miidera, in the neighboring town of Ōtsu; and Tōtarō went to Ōtsu to attend the festival. Among the multitude of women and young girls there assembled, he observed a person of extraordinary beauty. She seemed about sixteen years old; her face was fair and pure as snow; and the loveliness of her lips assured the beholder

---

* *Ryūgū* is also the name given to the whole of that fairy-realm beneath the sea, which figures in so many Japanese legends.

that their every utterance would sound "as sweet as the voice of a nightingale singing upon a plum-tree." Tōtarō fell in love with her at sight. When she left the temple he followed her at a respectful distance, and discovered that she and her mother were staying for a few days at a certain house in the neighboring village of Séta. By questioning some of the village folk, he was able also to learn that her name was Tamana; that she was unmarried; and that her family appeared to be unwilling that she should marry a man of ordinary rank,—for they demanded as a betrothal-gift a casket containing ten thousand jewels.*

Tōtarō returned home very much dismayed by this information. The more that he thought about the strange betrothal-gift demanded by the girl's parents, the more he felt that he could never expect to obtain her for his wife. Even supposing that there were as many as ten thousand jewels in the whole country, only a great prince could hope to procure them.

But not even for a single hour could Tōtarō banish from his mind the memory of that beautiful being. It haunted him so that he could neither eat nor sleep; and it seemed to become more and more vivid as the days went by. And at last he became ill,—so ill that he could not lift his head from the pillow. Then he sent for a doctor.

The doctor, after having made a careful examination, uttered an exclamation of surprise. "Almost any kind of sickness," he said, "can be cured by proper medical treatment, except the sickness of love.

---

* *Tama* in the original. This word *tama* has a multitude of meanings; and as here used it is quite as indefinite as our own terms "jewel," "gem," or "precious stone." Indeed, it is more indefinite, for it signifies also a bead of coral, a ball of crystal, a polished stone attached to a hairpin, etc., etc. Later on, however, I venture to render it by "ruby,"—for reasons which need no explanation.

Your ailment is evidently love-sickness. There is no cure for it. In ancient times Rōya-Ō Hakuyo died of that sickness; and you must prepare yourself to die as he died." So saying, the doctor went away, without even giving any medicine to Tōtarō.

About this time the Shark-Man that was living in the garden-pond heard of his master's sickness, and came into the house to wait upon Tōtarō. And he tended him with the utmost affection both by day and by night. But he did not know either the cause or the serious nature of the sickness until nearly a week later, when Tōtarō, thinking himself about to die, uttered these words of farewell:—

"I suppose that I have had the pleasure of caring for you thus long, because of some relation that grew up between us in a former state of existence. But now I am very sick indeed, and every day my sickness becomes worse; and my life is like the morning dew which passes away before the setting of the sun. For your sake, therefore, I am troubled in mind. Your existence has depended upon my care; and I fear that there will be no one to care for you and to feed you when I am dead. . . . My poor friend! . . . Alas! our hopes and our wishes are always disappointed in this unhappy world!"

No sooner had Tōtarō spoken these words than the Samébito uttered a strange wild cry of pain, and began to weep bitterly. And as he wept, great tears of blood streamed from his green eyes and rolled down his black cheeks and dripped upon the floor. And, falling, they were blood; but, having fallen, they became hard and bright and beautiful,—became jewels of inestimable price, rubies splendid as crimson fire. For when men of the sea weep, their tears become precious stones.

Then Tōtarō, beholding this marvel, was so amazed and overjoyed that his strength returned to him. He sprang from his bed, and began to pick up and to count the tears of the Shark-Man, crying out the while: "My sickness is cured! I shall live! I shall live!"

Therewith, the Shark-Man, greatly astonished, ceased to weep, and asked Tōtarō to explain this wonderful cure; and Tōtarō told him about the young person seen at Miidera, and about the extraordinary marriage-gift demanded by her family. "As I felt sure," added Tōtarō, "that I should never be able to get ten thousand jewels, I supposed that my suit would be hopeless. Then I became very unhappy, and at last fell sick. But now, because of your generous weeping, I have many precious stones; and I think that I shall be able to marry that girl. Only—there are not yet quite enough stones; and I beg that you will be good enough to weep a little more, so as to make up the full number required."

But at this request the Samébito shook his head, and answered in a tone of surprise and of reproach:—

"Do you think that I am like a harlot,—able to weep whenever I wish? Oh, no! Harlots shed tears in order to deceive men; but creatures of the sea cannot weep without feeling real sorrow. I wept for you because of the true grief that I felt in my heart at the thought that you were going to die. But now I cannot weep for you, because you have told me that your sickness is cured."

"Then what am I to do?" plaintively asked Tōtarō. "Unless I can get ten thousand jewels, I cannot marry the girl!"

The Samébito remained for a little while silent, as if thinking. Then he said:—

"Listen! To-day I cannot possibly weep any more. But to-morrow let us go together to the Long Bridge of Séta, taking with us some wine and some fish. We can rest for a time on the bridge; and while we are drinking the wine and eating the fish, I shall gaze in the direction of the Dragon-Palace, and try, by thinking of the happy days that I spent there, to make myself feel homesick—so that I can weep."

Tōtarō joyfully assented.

Next morning the two, taking plenty of wine and fish with them, went to the Séta bridge, and rested there, and feasted. After having drunk a great deal of wine, the Samébito began to gaze in the direction of the Dragon-Kingdom, and to think about the past. And gradually, under the softening influence of the wine, the memory of happier days filled his heart with sorrow, and the pain of homesickness came upon him, so that he could weep profusely. And the great red tears that he shed fell upon the bridge in a shower of rubies; and Tōtarō gathered them as they fell, and put them into a casket, and counted them until he had counted the full number of ten thousand. Then he uttered a shout of joy.

Almost in the same moment, from far away over the lake, a delightful sound of music was heard; and there appeared in the offing, slowly rising from the waters, like some fabric of cloud, a palace of the color of the setting sun.

At once the Samébito sprang upon the parapet of the bridge, and looked, and laughed for joy. Then, turning to Tōtarō, he said:—

"There must have been a general amnesty proclaimed in the Dragon-Realm; the Kings are calling me. So now I must bid you farewell. I am happy to have had one chance of befriending you in return for your goodness to me."

With these words he leaped from the bridge; and no man ever saw him again. But Tōtarō presented the casket of red jewels to the parents of Tamana, and so obtained her in marriage.

There was a young Samurai of Kyōto who had been reduced to poverty by the ruin of his lord, and found himself obliged to leave his home, and to take service with the Governor of a distant province. Before quitting the capital, this Samurai divorced his wife,—a good and beautiful woman,—under the belief that he could better obtain promotion by another alliance. He then married the daughter of a family of some distinction, and took her with him to the district whither he had been called.

But it was in the time of the thoughtlessness of youth, and the sharp experience of want, that the Samurai could not understand the worth of the affection so lightly cast away. His second marriage did not prove a happy one; the character of his new wife was hard and selfish; and he soon found every cause to think with regret of Kyōto days. Then he discovered that he still loved his first wife—loved her more than he could ever love the second; and he began to feel how unjust and how thankless he had been. Gradually his repentance deepened into a remorse that left him no peace of mind. Memories of the woman he had wronged—her gentle speech, her smiles, her dainty, pretty ways, her faultless patience— continually haunted him. Sometimes in dreams he saw her at her loom, weaving as when she toiled night and day to help him during the years of their distress: more often he saw her kneeling alone in the desolate little room where he had left her, veiling her tears with her poor worn sleeve. Even in the hours of official duty, his thoughts would wander back to her: then he would ask himself how she was living, what she was doing. Something in his heart assured him that she could not accept another husband, and that she never would refuse to pardon him. And he secretly resolved to seek her out as soon as he could return to Kyōto,—then to beg her forgiveness, to take her back, to do everything that a man could do to make atonement. But the years went by.

At last the Governor's official term expired, and the Samurai was free. "Now I will go back to my dear one," he vowed to himself. "Ah, what a cruelty,—what a folly to have divorced her!" He sent his second wife to her own people (she had given him no children); and hurrying to Kyōto, he went at once to seek his former companion,—not allowing himself even the time to change his traveling-garb.

When he reached the street where she used to live, it was late in the night,—the night of the tenth day of the ninth month;—and the city was silent as a cemetery. But a bright moon made everything visible; and he found the house without difficulty. It had a deserted look: tall weeds were growing on the roof. He knocked at the sliding-doors, and no one answered. Then, finding that the doors had not been fastened from within, he pushed them open, and entered. The front room was matless and empty: a chilly wind was blowing through crevices in the planking; and the moon shone through a ragged break in the wall of the alcove. Other rooms presented a like forlorn condition. The house, to all seeming, was unoccupied. Nevertheless, the Samurai determined to visit one other apartment at the further end of the dwelling,—a very small room that had been his wife's favorite resting-place. Approaching the sliding-screen that closed it, he was startled to perceive a glow within. He pushed the screen aside, and uttered a cry of joy; for he saw her there,—sewing by the light of a paper-lamp. Her eyes at the same instant met his own; and with a happy smile she greeted him,—asking only:—"When did you come back to Kyōto? How did you find your way here to me, through all those black rooms?" The years had not changed her. Still she seemed as fair and young as in his fondest memory of her;—but sweeter than any memory there came to him the music of her voice, with its trembling of pleased wonder.

Then joyfully he took his place beside her, and told her all:— how deeply he repented his selfishness,—how wretched he had been without her,—how constantly he had regretted her,—how long he had hoped and planned to make amends;—caressing her the while, and asking her forgiveness over and over again. She answered him, with loving gentleness, according to his heart's desire,—entreating him to cease all self-reproach. It was wrong, she said, that he should have allowed himself to suffer on her account: she had always felt that she was not worthy to be his wife. She knew that he had separated from her, notwithstanding, only because of poverty; and while he lived with her, he had always been kind; and she had never ceased to pray for his happiness. But even if there had been a reason for speaking of amends, this honorable visit would be ample amends;—what greater happiness than thus to see him again, though it were only for a moment? "Only for a moment!" he answered, with a glad laugh,—"say, rather, for the time of seven existences! My loved one, unless you forbid, I am coming back to live with you always—always—always! Nothing shall ever separate us again. Now I have means and friends: we need not fear poverty. Tomorrow my goods will be brought here; and my servants will come to wait upon you; and we shall make this house beautiful. . . . Tonight," he added, apologetically, "I came thus late—without even changing my dress—only because of the longing I had to see you, and to tell you this." She seemed greatly pleased by these words; and in her turn she told him about all that had happened in Kyōto since the time of his departure,—excepting her own sorrows, of which she sweetly refused to speak. They chatted far into the night: then she conducted him to a warmer room, facing south,—a room that had been their bridal chamber in former time. "Have you no one in the house to help you?" he asked, as she began to prepare the couch for him. "No," she answered, laughing cheerfully: "I could not afford a servant;—so I have been living all alone." "You will have plenty of servants tomorrow," he said,—"good servants,—and everything else that you need." They lay down to rest,—not to sleep: they had too much to tell each other;—and they talked of the past and the present and the future, until the dawn was gray. Then, involuntarily, the Samurai closed his eyes, and slept.

When he awoke, the daylight was streaming through the chinks of the sliding-shutters; and he found himself, to his utter amazement, lying upon the naked boards of a moldering floor. . . . Had he only dreamed a dream? No: she was there;—she slept. . . . He bent above her,—and looked,—and shrieked;—for the sleeper had no face! . . . Before him, wrapped in its grave-sheet only, lay the corpse of a woman,—a corpse so wasted that little remained save the bones, and the long black tangled hair.

Slowly,—as he stood shuddering and sickening in the sun,—the icy horror yielded to a despair so intolerable, a pain so atrocious,

that he clutched at the mocking shadow of a doubt. Feigning ignorance of the neighborhood, he ventured to ask his way to the house
in which his wife had lived.

"There is no one in that house," said the person questioned. "It
used to belong to the wife of a Samurai who left the city several
years ago. He divorced her in order to marry another woman before
he went away; and she fretted a great deal, and so became sick. She
had no relatives in Kyōto, and nobody to care for her; and she died
in the autumn of the same year,—on the tenth day of the ninth
month. . . ."

"I shall return in the early autumn," said Akana Soyëmon several hundred years ago,—when bidding good-bye to his brother by adoption, young Hasébé Samon. The time was spring; and the place was the village of Kato in the province of Harima. Akana was an Izumo samurai; and he wanted to visit his birthplace.

Hasébé said:—

"Your Izumo,—the Country of the Eight-Cloud Rising,*—is very distant. Perhaps it will therefore be difficult for you to promise to return here upon any particular day. But, if we were to know the exact day, we should feel happier. We could then prepare a feast of welcome; and we could watch at the gateway for your coming."

"Why, as for that," responded Akana, " I have been so much accustomed to travel that I can usually tell beforehand how long it will take me to reach a place; and I can safely promise you to be here upon a particular day. Suppose we say the day of the festival Chōyō?"

"That is the ninth day of the ninth month," said Hasébé;—"then the chrysanthemums will be in bloom, and we can go together to look at them. How pleasant! . . . So you promise to come back on the ninth day of the ninth month?"

---

* One of the old poetical names for the Province of Izumo or Unshus.

"On the ninth day of the ninth month," repeated Akana, smiling farewell. Then he strode away from the village of Kato in the province of Harima;—and Hasébé Samon and the mother of Hasébé looked after him with tears in their eyes.

"Neither the Sun nor the Moon," says an old Japanese proverb, "ever halt upon their journey." Swiftly the months went by; and the autumn came,—the season of chrysanthemums.

And early upon the morning of the ninth day of the ninth month Hasébé prepared to welcome his adopted brother. He made ready a feast of good things, bought wine, decorated the guest-room, and filled the vases of the alcove with chrysanthemums of two colors. Then his mother, watching him, said:—"The province of Izumo, my son, is more than one hundred *ri*[*] from this place; and the journey thence over the mountains is difficult and weary; and you cannot be sure that Akana will be able to come today. Would it not be better, before you take all this trouble, to wait for his coming?" "Nay, mother!" Hasébé made answer. "Akana promised to be here today: he could not break a promise. And if he were to see us beginning to make preparation after his arrival, he would know that we had doubted his word; and we should be put to shame."

The day was beautiful, the sky without a cloud, and the air so pure that the world seemed to be a thousand miles wider than usual. In the morning many travelers passed through the village—some of them samurai; and Hasébé, watching each as he came, more than once imagined that he saw Akana approaching. But the temple-bells sounded the hour of midday; and Akana did not appear. Through the afternoon also Hasébé watched and waited

---

[*] A *ri* is about equal to two and a half English miles.

in vain. The sun set; and still there was no sign of Akana. Nevertheless Hasébé remained at the gate, gazing down the road. Later his mother went to him, and said:—"The mind of a man, my son,—as our proverb declares—may change as quickly as the sky of autumn. But your chrysanthemum-flowers will still be fresh to-morrow. Better now to sleep; and in the morning you can watch again for Akana, if you wish." "Rest well, mother," returned Hasébé;—"but I still believe that he will come." Then the mother went to her own room; and Hasébé lingered at the gate. The night was pure as the day had been: all the sky throbbed with stars; and the white River of Heaven shimmered with unusual splendor. The village slept;—the silence was broken only by the noise of a little brook, and by the faraway barking of peasants' dogs. Hasébé still waited,—waited until he saw the thin moon sink behind the neighboring hills. Then at last he began to doubt and to fear. Just as he was about to re-enter the house, he perceived in the distance a tall man approaching,—very lightly and quickly; and in the next moment he recognized Akana.

"Oh!" cried Hasébé, springing to meet him—"I have been waiting for you from the morning until now! . . . So you really did keep your promise after all. . . . But you must be tired, poor brother!—come in;—everything is ready for you." He guided Akana to the place of honor in the guest-room, and hastened to trim the lights, which were burning low. "Mother," continued Hasébé, "felt a little tired this evening, and she has already gone to bed; but I shall awaken her presently." Akana shook his head, and made a little gesture of disapproval. "As you will, brother," said Hasébé; and he set warm food and wine before the traveler. Akana did not touch the food or the wine, but remained motionless and silent for a short

Umétsu Chūbei was a young samurai of great strength and courage. He was in the service of the Lord Tomura Jūdayū, whose castle stood upon a lofty hill in the neighborhood of Yokoté, in the province of Dewa. The house of the lord's retainers formed a small town at the base of the hill.

Umétsu was one of those selected for night-duty at the castle-gates. There were two night watches;—the first beginning at sunset and ending at midnight; the second beginning at midnight and ending at sunrise.

Once, when Umétsu happened to be on the second watch, he met with a strange adventure. While ascending the hill at midnight, to take his place on guard, he perceived a woman standing at the last upper turn of the winding road leading to the castle. She appeared to have a child in her arms, and to be waiting for somebody. Only the most extraordinary circumstances could account for the presence of a woman in that lonesome place at so late an hour; and Umétsu remembered that goblins were wont to assume feminine shapes after dark, in order to deceive and destroy men. He therefore doubted whether the seeming woman before him was really a human being; and when he saw her hasten towards him, as if to speak, he intended to pass her by without a word. But he was too much surprised to do so when the woman called him by name, and said, in a very sweet voice:—"Good Sir Umétsu, to-night I am in great trouble, and I have a most painful duty to perform: will you not kindly help me by holding this baby for one little moment?" And she held out the child to him.

Umétsu did not recognize the woman, who appeared to be very young: he suspected the charm of the strange voice, suspected a supernatural snare, suspected everything;—but he was naturally kind; and he felt that it would be unmanly to repress a kindly impulse through fear of goblins. Without replying, he took the child. "Please hold it till I come back," said the woman: "I shall return in a very little while." "I will hold it," he answered; and immediately the woman turned from him, and, leaving the road, sprang soundlessly down the hill so lightly and so quickly that he could scarcely believe his eyes. She was out of sight in a few seconds.

Umétsu then first looked at the child. It was very small, and appeared to have been just born. It was very still in his hands; and it did not cry at all.

Suddenly it seemed to be growing larger. He looked at it again. . . . No: it was the same small creature; and it had not even moved. Why had he imagined it was growing larger?

In another moment he knew why;—and he felt a chill strike through him. The child was not growing larger; *but it was growing heavier.* . . . At first it had seemed to weigh only seven or eight pounds: then its weight had gradually doubled—tripled—quadrupled. Now it could not weigh less than fifty pounds;—and still it was getting heavier and heavier. . . . A hundred pounds!—a hundred and fifty!—two hundred! . . . Umétsu knew that he had been deluded,—that he had not been speaking with any mortal woman,—that the child was not human. But he had made a promise; and a samurai was bound by his promise. So he kept the infant in his arms; and it continued to grow heavier and heavier . . .

two hundred and fifty!—three hundred!—four hundred pounds! . . . What was going to happen he could not imagine; but he resolved not to be afraid, and not to let the child go while his strength lasted. . . . Five hundred!—five hundred and fifty!—six hundred pounds! All his muscles began to quiver with the strain;—and still the weight increased. . . . "*Namu Amida Butsu!*" he groaned—"*Namu Amida Butsu!—Namu Amida Butsu!*" Even as he uttered the holy invocation for the third time, the weight passed away from him with a shock; and he stood stupefied with empty hands,—for the child had unaccountably disappeared. But almost in the same instant he saw the mysterious woman returning as quickly as she had gone. Still panting she came to him; and he then first saw that she was very fair;—but her brow dripped with sweat; and her sleeves were bound back with *tasuki* cords, as if she had been working hard.

"Kind Sir Umétsu," she said, "you do not know how great a service you have done me. I am the *Ujigami** of this place; and tonight one of my *Ujiko* found herself in the pains of childbirth, and prayed to me for aid. But the labor proved to be very difficult; and I soon saw that, by my own power alone, I might not be able to save her:—therefore I sought for the help of your strength and courage. And the child that I laid in your hands was the child that had not yet been born; and in the time that you first felt the child becoming heavier and heavier, the danger was very great,—for the Gates of Birth were closed. And when you felt the child become so heavy that you despaired of being able to bear the weight much

---

* *Ujigami* is the title given to the tutelary Shintō divinity of a parish or district. All persons living in that parish or district, and assisting in the maintenance of the temple (*miya*) of the deity, are called *Ujiko*.

longer,—in that same moment the mother seemed to be dead, and the family wept for her. Then you three times repeated the prayer, *Namu Amida Butsu!*—and the third time that you uttered it, the power of the Lord Buddha came to our aid and the Gates of Birth were opened. . . . And for that which you have done you shall be fitly rewarded. To a brave samurai no gift can be more serviceable than strength: therefore, not only to you, but likewise to your children and to your children's children, great strength shall be given." And, with this promise, the divinity disappeared.

Umétsu Chūbei, wondering greatly, resumed his way to the castle. At sunrise, on being relieved from duty, he proceeded as usual to wash his face and hands before making his morning prayer. But when he began to wring the towel which had served him, he was surprised to feel the tough material snap asunder in his hands. He attempted to twist together the separated portions; and again the stuff parted— like so much wet paper. He tried to wring the four thicknesses; and the result was the same. Presently, after handling various objects of bronze and of iron which yielded to his touch like clay, he understood that he had come into full possession of the great strength promised, and that he would have to be careful thenceforward when touching things, lest they should crumble in his fingers.

On returning home, he made inquiry as to whether any child had been born in the settlement during the night. Then he learned that a birth had actually taken place at the very hour of his adventure, and that the circumstances had been exactly as related to him by Ujigami.

The children of Umétsu Chūbei inherited their father's strength. Several of his descendants—all remarkably powerful men—were still living in the province of Dewa at the time when this story was written.

Nearly one thousand years ago there lived in the famous temple
called Miidera, at Ōtsu[*] in the province of Ōmi, a learned priest
named Kōgi. He was a great artist. He painted, with almost equal
skill, pictures of the Buddhas, pictures of beautiful scenery, and pictures of animals or birds; but he liked best to paint fishes. Whenever the weather was fair, and religious duty permitted, he would
go to Lake Biwa, and hire fishermen to catch fish for him, without
injuring them in any way, so that he could paint them afterwards
as they swam about in a large vessel of water. After having made
pictures of them, and having fed them like pets, he would set them
free again,—taking them back to the lake himself. His pictures of
fish at last became so famous that people traveled from great distances to see them. But the most wonderful of all his drawings of
fish was not drawn from life, but was made from the memory of a
dream. For one day, as he sat by the lake-side to watch the fishes
swimming, Kōgi had fallen into a doze, and had dreamed that he
was playing with the fishes under the water. After he awoke, the
memory of the dream remained so clear that he was able to paint

[*] The town of Ōtsu stands on the shore of the great Lake of Ōmi,—usually called
Lake Biwa;—and the temple Miidera is situated upon a hill overlooking the water. Miidera
was founded in the seventh century, but has been several times rebuilt: the present structure dates back to the latter part of the seventeenth century.

it; and this painting, which he hung up in the alcove of his own room in the temple, he called "Dream-Carp."

Kōgi could never be persuaded to sell any of his pictures of fish. He was willing to part with his drawings of landscapes, of birds, or of flowers; but he said that he would not sell a picture of living fish to any one who was cruel enough to kill or to eat fish. And as the persons who wanted to buy his paintings were all fish-eaters, their offers of money could not tempt him.

One summer Kōgi fell sick; and after a week's illness he lost all power of speech and movement so that he seemed to be dead. But after his funeral service had been performed, his disciples discovered some warmth in the body, and decided to postpone the burial for a while, and to keep watch by the seeming corpse. In the afternoon of the same day he suddenly revived, and questioned the watchers, asking:—

"How long have I remained without knowledge of the world?"

"More than three days," an acolyte made answer. "We thought that you were dead; and this morning your friends and parishioners assembled in the temple for your funeral service. We performed the service; but afterwards, finding that your body was not altogether cold, we put off the burial; and now we are very glad that we did so."

Kōgi nodded approvingly: then he said:—

"I want some one of you to go immediately to the house of Taira no Suké, where the young men are having a feast at the present moment—they are eating fish and drinking wine,—and say to them:—'Our master has revived; and he begs that you will be so good as to leave your feast, and to call upon him without delay, because he has a wonderful story to tell you. . . .'

"At the same time"—continued Kōgi—"observe what Suké and his brothers are doing;—see whether they are not feasting as I say."

Then an acolyte went at once to the house of Taira no Suké, and was surprised to find that Suké and his brother Jūrō, with their attendant, Kamori, were having a feast, just as Kōgi had said. But, on receiving the message, all three immediately left their fish and wine, and hastened to the temple. Kōgi, lying upon the couch to which he had been removed, received them with a smile of welcome; and, after some pleasant words had been exchanged, he said to Suké:—

"Now, my friend, please reply to some questions that I am going to ask you. First of all, kindly tell me whether you did not buy a fish today from the fisherman Bunshi."

"Why, yes," replied Suké—"but how did you know?"

"Please wait a moment," said the priest. . . . "That fisherman Bunshi today entered your gate, with a fish three feet long in his basket: it was early in the afternoon, just after you and Jūrō had begun a game of *go*;—and Kamori was watching the game, and eating a peach—was he not?"

"That is true," exclaimed Suké and Kamori together, with increasing surprise.

"And when Kamori saw that big fish," proceeded Kōgi, "he agreed to buy it at once; and, besides paying the price of the fish, he also gave Bunshi some peaches, in a dish, and three cups of wine. Then the cook was called; and he came and looked at the fish, and admired it; and then, by your order, he sliced it and prepared it for your feast. . . . Did not all this happen just as I have said?"

"Yes," responded Suké; "but we are very much astonished that you should know what happened in our house today. Please tell us how you learned these matters."

"Well, now for my story," said the priest. "You are aware that almost everybody believed me to be dead;—you yourselves attended my funeral service. But I did not think, three days ago, that I was at all dangerously ill! I remember only that I felt weak and very hot, and that I wanted to go out into the air to cool myself. And I thought that I got up from my bed, with a great effort, and went out,—supporting myself with a stick. . . . Perhaps this may have been imagination; but you will presently be able to judge the truth for yourselves: I am going to relate everything exactly as it appeared to happen. . . . As soon as I got outside of the house, into the bright air, I began to feel quite light,—light as a bird flying away from the net or the basket in which it has been confined. I wandered on and on till I reached the lake; and the water looked so beautiful and blue that I felt a great desire to have a swim. I took off my clothes, and jumped in, and began to swim about; and I was astonished to find that I could swim very fast and very skillfully,—although before my sickness I had always been a very poor swimmer. . . . You think that I am only telling you a foolish dream—but listen! . . . While I was wondering at this new skill of mine, I perceived many beautiful fishes swimming below me and around me; and I felt suddenly envious of their happiness,—reflecting that, no matter how good a swimmer a man may become, he never can enjoy himself under the water as a fish can. Just then, a very big fish lifted its head above the surface in front of me, and spoke to me with the voice of a man, saying:—'That wish of yours can very easily be satisfied: please wait there a moment!' The fish then went down, out of sight; and I waited. After a few minutes there came up, from the bottom of the lake,—riding on the back of the same big fish that had spoken to me,—a man wearing the headdress and the ceremonial robes of a prince; and the man said to me:—'I come to you with a message from the Dragon-King, who knows of your desire to enjoy for a little time the condition of a fish. As you have saved the lives of many fish, and have always shown compassion to living creatures, the God now bestows upon you the attire of the Golden Carp, so that you will be able to enjoy the pleasures of the Water-World. But you must be very careful not to eat any fish, or any food prepared from fish,—no matter how nice may be the smell of it—and you must also take great care not to get caught by the fishermen, or to hurt your body in any way.' With these words, the messenger and his fish went below and vanished in the deep water. I looked at myself, and saw that my whole body had become covered with scales that shone like gold;—I saw that I had fins;—I found that I had actually been changed into a Golden Carp. Then I knew that I could swim wherever I pleased.

"Thereafter it seemed to me that I swam away, and visited many beautiful places. (*Here, in the original narrative, are introduced some verses describing the Eight Famous Attractions of the Lake of Ōmi,—"Ōmi-Hakkei."*) Sometimes i was satisfied only to look at the sunlight dancing over the blue water, or to admire the beautiful reflection of hills and trees upon still surfaces sheltered from the wind. . . . I remember especially the coast of an island—either Okitsushima or Chikubushima—reflected in the water like a red wall. . . . Sometimes I would approach the shore so closely that I could see the faces and hear the voices of people passing by; sometimes I would sleep on the water until startled by the sound of approaching oars. At night there were beautiful moonlight-views; but I was frightened more than once by the approaching torchfires of the fishing-boats of Katasé. When the weather was bad, I would go below,—far down,—even a thousand feet,—and play at the bottom of the lake. But after two or three days of this wandering pleasure, I began to feel very hungry; and I returned to this neighborhood in the hope of finding something to eat. Just at that time the fisherman Bunshi happened to be fishing; and I approached the hook which he had let down into the water. There was some fish-food upon it that was good to smell. I remembered in the same moment the warning of the Dragon-King, and swam away, saying to myself:—'In any event I must not eat food containing fish;—I am a disciple of the Buddha.' Yet after a little while my hunger became so intense that I could not resist the temptation; and I swam back again to the hook, thinking,—'Even if Bunshi should catch me, he would not hurt me;—he is my old friend.' I was not able to loosen the bait from the hook; and the pleasant smell of the food was too much for my patience; and I swallowed the whole thing at a gulp. Immediately after I did so, Bunshi pulled in his line, and caught me. I cried out to him, 'What are you doing?—you hurt me!'—but he did not seem to hear me, and he quickly put a string through my jaws. Then he threw me into his basket, and took me to your house. When the basket was opened there, I saw you and Jūrō playing *go* in the south room, and Kamori watching you—eating a peach the while. All of you presently came out upon the veranda to look at me; and you were delighted to see such a big fish. I called out to you as loud as I could:—'I am not a fish!—I am Kōgi—Kōgi the priest! Please let me go back to my temple!' But you clapped your hands for gladness, and paid no attention to my words. Then your cook carried me into the kitchen, and threw me down violently upon a cutting-board, where a terribly sharp knife was lying. With his left hand he pressed me down, and with his right hand he took up that knife,—and I screamed to him:—'How can you kill me so cruelly! I am a disciple of the Buddha!—help! help!' But in the same instant I felt his knife dividing me—a frightful pain!—and then I suddenly awoke, and found myself here in the temple."

When the priest had thus finished his story, the brothers wondered at it; and Suké said to him:—"I now remember noticing that the jaws of the fish were moving all the time that we were looking at it; but we did not hear any voice. . . . Now I must send a servant to the house with orders to throw the remainder of that fish into the lake."

Kōgi soon recovered from his illness, and lived to paint many more pictures. It is related that long after his death, some of his fish-pictures once happened to fall into the lake, and that the figures of the fish immediately detached themselves from the silk or the paper upon which they had been painted, and swam away!

During the period of Tenshō* there lived, in one of the northern districts of Kyōto, an old man whom the people called Kwashin Koji. He wore a long white beard, and was always dressed like a Shintō priest; but he made his living by exhibiting Buddhist pictures and by preaching Buddhist doctrine. Every fine day he used to go to the grounds of the temple Gion, and there suspend to some tree a large kakémono on which were depicted the punishments of the various hells. This kakémono was so wonderfully painted that all things represented in it seemed to be real; and the old man would discourse to the people crowding to see it, and explain to them the Law of Cause and Effect,—pointing out with a Buddhist staff (*nyoi*), which he always carried, each detail of the different torments, and exhorting everybody to follow the teachings of the Buddha. Multitudes assembled to look at the picture and to hear the old man preach about it; and sometimes the mat which he spread before him, to receive contributions, was covered out of sight by the heaping of coins thrown upon it.

Oda Nobunaga was at that time ruler of Kyōto and of the surrounding provinces. One of his retainers, named Arakawa, during a visit to the temple of Gion, happened to see the picture being

---

* The period of Tenshō lasted from 1573 to 1591 (A.D.). The death of the great captain, Oda Nobunaga, who figures in this story, occurred in 1582.

displayed there; and he afterwards talked about it at the palace. Nobunaga was interested by Arakawa's description, and sent orders to Kwashin Koji to come at once to the palace, and to bring the picture with him.

When Nobunaga saw the kakémono he was not able to conceal his surprise at the vividness of the work: the demons and the tortured spirits actually appeared to move before his eyes; and he heard voices crying out of the picture; and the blood there represented seemed to be really flowing,—so that he could not help putting out his finger to feel if the painting was wet. But the finger was not stained,—for the paper proved to be perfectly dry. More and more astonished, Nobunaga asked who had made the wonderful picture. Kwashin Koji answered that it had been painted by the famous Oguri Sōtan,[*]—after he had performed the rite of self-purification every day for a hundred days, and practiced great austerities, and made earnest prayer for inspiration to the divine Kwannon of Kiyomidzu Temple.

Observing Nobunaga's evident desire to possess the kakémono, Arakawa then asked Kwashin Koji whether he would "offer it up," as a gift to the great lord. But the old man boldly answered:—"This painting is the only object of value that I possess; and I am able to make a little money by showing it to the people. Were I now to present this picture to the lord, I should deprive myself of the only means which I have to make my living. However, if the lord be greatly desirous to possess it, let him pay me for it the sum of one hundred ryō of gold. With that amount of money I should be able to engage in some profitable business. Otherwise, I must refuse to give up the picture."

---

[*] Oguri Sōtan was a great religious artist who flourished in the early part of the fifteenth century. He became a Buddhist priest in the later years of his life.

Nobunaga did not seem to be pleased at this reply; and he remained silent. Arakawa presently whispered something in the ear of the lord, who nodded assent; and Kwashin Koji was then dismissed, with a small present of money.

But when the old man left the palace, Arakawa secretly followed him,—hoping for a chance to get the picture by foul means. The chance came; for Kwashin Koji happened to take a road leading directly to the heights beyond the town. When he reached a certain lonesome spot at the foot of the hills, where the road made a sudden turn, he was seized by Arakawa, who said to him:—"Why were you so greedy as to ask a hundred ryō of gold for that picture? Instead of a hundred ryō of gold, I am now going to give you one piece of iron three feet long." Then Arakawa drew his sword, and killed the old man, and took the picture.

The next day Arakawa presented the kakémono—still wrapped up as Kwashin Koji had wrapped it before leaving the palace—to Oda Nobunaga, who ordered it to be hung up forthwith. But, when it was unrolled, both Nobunaga and his retainer were astounded to find that there was no picture at all—nothing but a blank surface. Arakawa could not explain how the original painting had disappeared; and as he had been guilty—whether willingly or unwillingly—of deceiving his master, it was decided that he should be punished. Accordingly he was sentenced to remain in confinement for a considerable time.

Scarcely had Arakawa completed his term of imprisonment, when news was brought to him that Kwashin Koji was exhibiting the famous picture in the grounds of Kitano Temple. Arakawa could hardly believe his ears; but the information inspired him with a vague hope that he might be able, in some way or other, to secure the kakémono, and thereby redeem his recent fault. So he quickly assembled some of his followers, and hurried to the temple; but when he reached it he was told that Kwashin Koji had gone away.

Several days later, word was brought to Arakawa that Kwashin Koji was exhibiting the picture at Kiyomidzu Temple, and preaching about it to an immense crowd. Arakawa made all haste to Kiyomidzu; but he arrived there only in time to see the crowd disperse,—for Kwashin Koji had again disappeared.

At last one day Arakawa unexpectedly caught sight of Kwashin Koji in a wine-shop, and there captured him. The old man only laughed good-humoredly on finding himself seized, and said:—"I will go with you; but please wait until I drink a little wine." To this request Arakawa made no objection; and Kwashin Koji thereupon drank, to the amazement of the bystanders, twelve bowls of wine. After drinking the twelfth he declared himself satisfied; and Arakawa ordered him to be bound with a rope, and taken to Nobunaga's residence.

In the court of the palace Kwashin Koji was examined at once by the Chief Officer, and sternly reprimanded. Finally the Chief Officer said to him:—"It is evident that you have been deluding people by magical practices; and for this offense alone you deserve to be heavily punished. However, if you will now respectfully offer up that picture to the Lord Nobunaga, we shall this time overlook your fault. Otherwise we shall certainly inflict upon you a very severe punishment."

At this menace Kwashin Koji laughed in a bewildered way, and exclaimed:—"It is not I who have been guilty of deluding people." Then, turning to Arakawa, he cried out:—"You are the deceiver! You wanted to flatter the lord by giving him that picture; and you tried to kill me in order to steal it. Surely, if there be any such thing as crime, that was a crime! As luck would have it, you did not succeed in killing me; but if you had succeeded, as you wished, what would you have been able to plead in excuse for such an act? You stole the picture, at all events. The picture that I now have is only a copy. And after you stole the picture, you changed your mind about giving it to Lord Nobunaga; and you devised a plan to keep it for yourself. So you gave a blank kakémono to Lord Nobunaga; and, in order to conceal your secret act and purpose, you pretended that I had deceived you by substituting a blank kakémono for the real one. Where the real picture now is, I do not know. You probably do."

At these words Arakawa became so angry that he rushed towards the prisoner, and would have struck him but for the interference of the guards. And this sudden outburst of anger caused the Chief Officer to suspect that Arakawa was not altogether innocent. He ordered Kwashin Koji to be taken to prison for the time being; and he then proceeded to question Arakawa closely. Now Arakawa was naturally slow of speech; and on this occasion, being greatly excited, he could scarcely speak at all; and he stammered, and contradicted himself, and betrayed every sign of guilt. Then the Chief Officer ordered that Arakawa should be beaten with a stick until he told the truth. But it was not possible for him even to seem to tell the truth. So he was beaten with a bamboo until his senses departed from him, and he lay as if dead.

Kwashin Koji was told in the prison about what had happened to Arakawa; and he laughed. But after a little while he said to the jailer:—"Listen! That fellow Arakawa really behaved like a rascal; and I purposely brought this punishment upon him, in order to correct his evil inclinations. But now please say to the Chief Officer that Arakawa must have been ignorant of the truth, and that I shall explain the whole matter satisfactorily."

Then Kwashin Koji was again taken before the Chief Officer, to whom he made the following declaration:—"In any picture of real excellence there must be a ghost; and such a picture, having a will of its own, may refuse to be separated from the person who gave it life, or even from its rightful owner. There are many stories to prove that really great pictures have souls. It is well known that some sparrows, painted upon a sliding-screen (*fusuma*) by Hōgen Yenshin, once flew away, leaving blank the spaces which they had occupied upon the surface. Also it is well known that a horse, painted upon a certain kakémono, used to go out at night to eat grass. Now, in this present case, I believe the truth to be that, inasmuch as the Lord Nobunaga never became the rightful owner of my kakémono, the picture voluntarily vanished from the paper when it was unrolled in his presence. But if you will give me the price that I first asked,—one hundred ryō of gold,—I think that the painting will then reappear, of its own accord, upon the now blank paper. At all events, let us try! There is nothing to risk,—since, if the picture does not reappear, I shall at once return the money."

On hearing of these strange assertions, Nobunaga ordered the hundred ryō to be paid, and came in person to observe the result. The kakémono was then unrolled before him; and, to the amazement of all present, the painting reappeared, with all its details. But the colors seemed to have faded a little; and the figures of the souls and the demons did not look really alive, as before. Perceiving this difference, the lord asked Kwashin Koji to explain the reason of it; and Kwashin Koji replied:—"The value of the painting, as you first saw it, was the value of a painting beyond all price. But the value of the painting, as you now see it, represents exactly what you paid for it,—one hundred ryō of gold. . . . How could it be otherwise?" On hearing this answer, all present felt that it would be worse than useless to oppose the old man any further. He was immediately set at liberty; and Arakawa was also liberated, as he had more than expiated his fault by the punishment which he had undergone.

Now Arakawa had a younger brother named Buichi,—also a retainer in the service of Nobunaga. Buichi was furiously angry because Arakawa had been beaten and imprisoned; and he resolved to kill Kwashin Koji. Kwashin Koji no sooner found himself again at liberty than he went straight to a wine-shop, and called for wine. Buichi rushed after him into the shop, struck him down, and cut off his head. Then, taking the hundred ryō that had been paid to the old man, Buichi wrapped up the head and the gold together in a cloth, and hurried home to show them to Arakawa. But when he unfastened the cloth he found, instead of the head, only an empty wine-gourd, and only a lump of filth instead of the gold— . . . And the bewilderment of the brothers was presently increased by the information that the headless body had disappeared from the wine-shop,—none could say how or when.

Nothing more was heard of Kwashin Koji until about a month later, when a drunken man was found one evening asleep in the gateway of Lord Nobunaga's palace, and snoring so loudly that every snore sounded like the rumbling of distant thunder. A retainer discovered that the drunkard was Kwashin Koji. For this insolent offense, the old fellow was at once seized and thrown into the prison. But he did not awaken; and in the prison he continued to sleep without interruption for ten days and ten nights,—all the while snoring so that the sound could be heard to a great distance.

About this time, the Lord Nobunaga came to his death through the treachery of one of his captains, Akéchi Mitsuhidé, who thereupon usurped rule. But Mitsuhidé's power endured only for a period of twelve days.

Now when Mitsuhidé became master of Kyōto, he was told of the case of Kwashin Koji; and he ordered that the prisoner should be brought before him. Accordingly Kwashin Koji was summoned into the presence of the new lord; but Mitsuhidé spoke to him kindly, treated him as a guest, and commanded that a good dinner should be served to him. When the old man had eaten, Mitsuhidé said to him:—"I have heard that you are very fond of wine;— how much wine can you drink at a single sitting?" Kwashin Koji answered:—"I do not really know how much; I stop drinking only when I feel intoxication coming on." Then the lord set a great wine-cup* before Kwashin Koji, and told a servant to fill the cup as often as the old man wished. And Kwashin Koji emptied the great cup ten times in succession, and asked for more; but the servant made answer that the wine-vessel was exhausted. All present were astounded by this drinking-feat; and the lord asked Kwashin Koji, "Are you not yet satisfied, Sir?" "Well, yes," replied Kwashin Koji, "I am somewhat satisfied;—and now, in return for your august kindness, I shall display a little of my art. Be therefore so good as to observe that screen." He pointed to a large eight-folding screen upon which were painted the Eight Beautiful Views of the Lake of Ōmi (*Ōmi-Hakkei*); and everybody looked at the screen. In one of the views the artist had represented, far away on the lake, a man rowing a boat,—the boat occupying, upon the surface of

---

* The term "bowl" would better indicate the kind of vessel to which the storyteller refers. Some of the so-called cups, used on festival occasions, were very large,—shallow lacquered basins capable of holding considerably more than a quart. To empty one of the largest size, at a draught, was considered no small feat.

the screen, a space of less than an inch in length. Kwashin Koji then waved his hand in the direction of the boat; and all saw the boat suddenly turn, and begin to move toward the foreground of the picture. It grew rapidly larger and larger as it approached; and presently the features of the boatman became clearly distinguishable. Still the boat drew nearer,—always becoming larger,—until it appeared to be only a short distance away. And, all of a sudden, the water of the lake seemed to overflow,—out of the picture into the room;—and the room was flooded; and the spectators girded up their robes in haste, as the water rose above their knees. In the same moment the boat appeared to glide out of the screen,—a real fishing-boat;—and the creaking of the single oar could be heard. Still the flood in the room continued to rise, until the spectators were standing up to their girdles in water. Then the boat came close up to Kwashin Koji; and Kwashin Koji climbed into it; and the boatman turned about, and began to row away very swiftly. And, as the boat receded, the water in the room began to lower rapidly,—seeming to ebb back into the screen. No sooner had the boat passed the apparent foreground of the picture than the room was dry again! But still the painted vessel appeared to glide over the painted water,—retreating farther into the distance, and ever growing smaller,—till at last it dwindled to a dot in the offing. And then it disappeared altogether; and Kwashin Koji disappeared with it. He was never again seen in Japan.

More than seven hundred years ago, at Dan-no-ura, in the Straits of Shimonoséki, was fought the last battle of the long contest between the Heiké, or Taira clan, and the Genji, or Minamoto clan. There the Heiké perished utterly, with their women and children, and their infant emperor likewise—now remembered as Antoku Tennō. And that sea and shore have been haunted for seven hundred years.... Elsewhere I told you about the strange crabs found there, called Heiké crabs, which have human faces on their backs, and are said to be the spirits of the Heiké warriors. But there are many strange things to be seen and heard along that coast. On dark nights thousands of ghostly fires hover about the beach, or flit above the waves,—pale lights which the fishermen call *Oni-bi*, or demon-fires; and, whenever the winds are up, a sound of great shouting comes from that sea, like a clamor of battle.

In former years the Heiké were much more restless than they now are. They would rise about ships passing in the night, and try to sink them; and at all times they would watch for swimmers, to pull them down. It was in order to appease those dead that the Buddhist temple, Amidaji, was built at Akamagaséki.* A cemetery also was made close by, near the beach; and within it were set up monuments inscribed with the names of the drowned emperor and

---

* Or Shimonoséki. The town is also known by the name of Bakkan.

of his great vassals; and Buddhist services were regularly performed there, on behalf of the spirits of them. After the temple had been built, and the tombs erected, the Heiké gave less trouble than before; but they continued to do queer things at intervals,—proving that they had not found the perfect peace.

Some centuries ago there lived at Akamagaséki a blind man named Hōichi, who was famed for his skill in recitation and in playing upon the *biwa*.* From childhood he had been trained to recite and to play; and while yet a lad he had surpassed his teachers. As a professional *biwa-hōshi* he became famous chiefly by his recitations of the history of the Heiké and the Genji; and it is said that when he sang the song of the battle of Dan-no-ura "even the goblins (*kijin*) could not refrain from tears."

At the outset of his career, Hōichi was very poor; but he found a good friend to help him. The priest of the Amidaji was fond of poetry and music; and he often invited Hōichi to the temple, to play and recite. Afterwards, being much impressed by the wonderful skill of the lad, the priest proposed that Hōichi should make the temple his home; and this offer was gratefully accepted. Hōichi was given a room in the temple-building; and, in return for food and lodging, he was required only to gratify the priest with a musical performance on certain evenings, when otherwise disengaged.

One summer night the priest was called away, to perform a Buddhist service at the house of a dead parishioner; and he went there with his acolyte, leaving Hōichi alone in the temple. It was a hot

---

* The *biwa*, a kind of four-stringed lute, is chiefly used in musical recitative. Formerly the professional minstrels who recited the *Heiké-Monogatari* and other tragical histories were called *biwa-hōshi*, or "lute priests," as well as blind barbers, had their heads shaven, like Buddhist priests. The *biwa* is played with a kind of plectrum, called *bachi*, usually made of horn.

night; and the blind man sought to cool himself on the verandah before his sleeping-room. The verandah overlooked a small garden in the rear of the Amidaji. There Hōichi waited for the priest's return, and tried to relieve his solitude by practicing upon his biwa. Midnight passed; and the priest did not appear. But the atmosphere was still too warm for comfort within doors; and Hōichi remained outside. At last he heard steps approaching from the back gate. Somebody crossed the garden, advanced to the verandah, and halted directly in front of him—but it was not the priest. A deep voice called the blind man's name—abruptly and unceremoniously, in the manner of a samurai summoning an inferior:—

"Hōichi!"

Hōichi was much too startled, for the moment, to respond; and the voice called again, in a tone of harsh command,—

"Hōichi!"

"*Hai!*"* answered the blind man, frightened by the menace in the voice,—"I am blind!—I cannot know who calls!"

"There is nothing to fear," the stranger exclaimed, speaking more gently. "I am stopping near this temple, and have been sent to you with a message. My present lord, a person of exceedingly high rank, is now staying in Akamagaséki, with many noble attendants. He wished to view the scene of the battle of Dan-no-ura; and today he visited that place. Having heard of your skill in reciting the story of the battle, he now desires to hear your performance: so you will take your biwa and come with me at once to the house where the august assembly is waiting."

In those times, the order of a samurai was not to be lightly disobeyed. Hōichi donned his sandals, took his biwa, and went away

---

* A response to show that one has heard and is listening attentively.

with the stranger, who guided him deftly, but obliged him to walk very fast. The hand that guided was iron; and the clank of the warrior's stride proved him fully armed,—probably some palace-guard on duty. Hōichi's first alarm was over: he began to imagine himself in good luck;—for, remembering the retainer's assurance about a "person of exceedingly high rank," he thought that the lord who wished to hear the recitation could not be less than a daimyō of the first class. Presently the samurai halted; and Hōichi became aware that they had arrived at a large gateway;—and he wondered, for he could not remember any large gate in that part of the town, except the main gate of the Amidaji. "*Kaimon!*"[*] the samurai called,—and there was a sound of unbarring; and the twain passed on. They traversed a space of garden, and halted again before some entrance; and the retainer cried in a loud voice, "Within there! I have brought Hōichi." Then came sounds of feet hurrying, and screens sliding, and rain-doors opening, and voices of women in converse. By the language of the women Hōichi knew them to be domestics in some noble household; but he could not imagine to what place he had been conducted. Little time was allowed him for conjecture. After he had been helped to mount several stone steps, upon the last of which he was told to leave his sandals, a woman's hand guided him along interminable reaches of polished planking, and round pillared angles too many to remember, and over widths amazing of matted floor,—into the middle of some vast apartment. There he thought that many great people were assembled: the sound of the rustling of silk was like the sound of leaves in a forest. He heard also a great humming of voices,—talking in undertones; and the speech was the speech of courts.

---

[*] A respectful term, signifying the opening of a gate. It was used by samurai when calling to the guards at a lord's gate for admission.

Hōichi was told to put himself at ease, and he found a kneeling-cushion ready for him. After having taken his place upon it, and tuned his instrument, the voice of a woman—whom he divined to be the *Rōjo*, or matron in charge of the female service—addressed him, saying,—

"It is now required that the history of the Héike be recited, to the accompaniment of the biwa."

Now the entire recital would have required a time of many nights: therefore Hōichi ventured a question:—

"As the whole of the story is not soon told, what portion is it augustly desired that I now recite?"

The woman's voice made answer:—

"Recite the story of the battle at Dan-no-ura,—for the pity of it is the most deep."*

Then Hōichi lifted up his voice, and chanted the chant of the fight on the bitter sea,—wonderfully making his biwa to sound like the straining of oars and the rushing of ships, the whirr and the hissing of arrows, the shouting and trampling of men, the crashing of steel upon helmets, the plunging of slain in the flood. And to the left and right of him, in the pauses of his playing, he could hear voices murmuring praise:"How marvelous an artist!"—"Never in our own province was playing heard like this!"—"Not in all the empire is there another singer like Hōichi!" Then fresh courage came to him, and he played and sang yet better than before; and a hush of wonder deepened about him. But when at last he came to tell the fate of the fair and helpless,—the piteous perishing of the women and children,—and the death-leap of Nii-no-Ama, with the imperial

* Or the phrase might be rendered, "for the pity of that part is the deepest." The Japanese word for pity in the original text is *awaré*.

infant in her arms,—then all the listeners uttered together one long, long shuddering cry of anguish; and thereafter they wept and wailed so loudly and so wildly that the blind man was frightened by the violence and grief that he had made. For much time the sobbing and the wailing continued. But gradually the sounds of lamentation died away; and again, in the great stillness that followed, Hōichi heard the voice of the woman whom he supposed to be the *Rōjo*.

She said:—

"Although we had been assured that you were a very skillful player upon the biwa, and without an equal in recitative, we did not know that anyone could be so skillful as you have proved yourself tonight. Our lord has been pleased to say that he intends to bestow upon you a fitting reward. But he desires that you shall perform before him once every night for the next six nights—after which time he will probably make his august return-journey. Tomorrow night, therefore, you are to come here at the same hour. The retainer who tonight conducted you will be sent for you. . . . There is another matter about which I have been ordered to inform you. It is required that you shall speak to no one of your visits here, during the time of our lord's august sojourn at Akamagaséki. As he is traveling incognito,* he commands that no mention of these things be made. . . . You are now free to go back to your temple."

After Hōichi had duly expressed his thanks, a woman's hand conducted him to the entrance of the house, where the same retainer, who had before guided him, was waiting to take him home. The retainer led him to the verandah at the rear of the temple, and there bade him farewell.

---

* "Traveling incognito" is at least the meaning of the original phrase—"making a disguised august-journey" (*shinobi no go-ryokō*).

It was almost dawn when Hōichi returned; but his absence from the temple had not been observed,—as the priest, coming back at a very late hour, had supposed him asleep. During the day Hōichi was able to take some rest; and he said nothing about his strange adventure. In the middle of the following night the samurai again came for him, and led him to the august assembly, where he gave another recitation with the same success that had attended his previous performance. But during this second visit his absence from the temple was accidentally discovered; and after his return in the morning he was summoned to the presence of the priest, who said to him, in a tone of kindly reproach:—

"We have been very anxious about you, friend Hōichi. To go out, blind and alone, at so late an hour, is dangerous. Why did you go without telling us? I could have ordered a servant to accompany you. And where have you been?"

Hōichi answered, evasively,—

"Pardon me kind friend! I had to attend to some private business; and I could not arrange the matter at any other hour."

The priest was surprised, rather than pained, by Hōichi's reticence: he felt it to be unnatural, and suspected something wrong. He feared that the blind lad had been bewitched or deluded by some evil spirits. He did not ask any more questions; but he privately instructed the men-servants of the temple to keep watch upon Hōichi's movements, and to follow him in case he should again leave the temple after dark.

On the very next night, Hōichi was seen to leave the temple; and the servants immediately lighted their lanterns, and followed after him. But it was a rainy night, and very dark; and before the temple-folks could get to the roadway, Hōichi had disappeared. Evidently he had walked very fast,—a strange thing, considering his blindness;

for the road was in a bad condition. The men hurried through the streets, making inquiries at every house which Hōichi was accustomed to visit; but nobody could give them any news of him. At last, as they were returning to the temple by way of the shore, they were startled by the sound of a biwa, furiously played, in the cemetery of the Amidaji. Except for some ghostly fires—such as usually flitted there on dark nights—all was blackness in that direction. But the men at once hastened to the cemetery; and there, by the help of their lanterns, they discovered Hōichi,—sitting alone in the rain before the memorial tomb of Antoku Tennō, making his biwa resound, and loudly chanting the chant of the battle of Dan-no-ura. And behind him, and about him, and everywhere above the tombs, the fires of the dead were burning, like candles. Never before had so great a host of Oni-bi appeared in the sight of mortal man. . . .

"Hōichi San!—Hōichi San!" the servants cried,—"you are bewitched! . . . Hōichi San!"

But the blind man did not seem to hear. Strenuously he made his biwa to rattle and ring and clang;—more and more wildly he chanted the chant of the battle of Dan-no-ura. They caught hold of him;—they shouted into his ear,—

"Hōichi San!—Hōichi San!—come home with us at once!"

Reprovingly he spoke to them:—

"To interrupt me in such a manner, before this august assembly, will not be tolerated."

Whereat, in spite of the weirdness of the thing, the servants could not help laughing. Sure that he had been bewitched, they now seized him, and pulled him up on his feet, and by main force hurried him back to the temple,—where he was immediately relieved of his wet clothes, by order of the priest. Then the priest insisted upon a full explanation of his friend's astonishing behavior.

Hōichi long hesitated to speak. But at last, finding that his conduct had really alarmed and angered the good priest, he decided to abandon his reserve; and he related everything that had happened from the time of first visit of the samurai.

The priest said:—

"Hōichi, my poor friend, you are now in great danger! How unfortunate that you did not tell me all this before! Your wonderful skill in music has indeed brought you into strange trouble. By this time you must be aware that you have not been visiting any house whatever, but have been passing your nights in the cemetery, among the tombs of the Heiké;—and it was before the memorial-tomb of Antoku Tennō that our people tonight found you, sitting in the rain. All that you have been imagining was illusion—except the calling of the dead. By once obeying them, you have put yourself in their power. If you obey them again, after what has already occurred, they will tear you in pieces. But they would have destroyed you, sooner or later, in any event. . . . Now I shall not be able to remain with you tonight: I am called away to perform another service. But, before I go, it will be necessary to protect your body by writing holy texts upon it."

Before sundown the priest and his acolyte stripped Hōichi: then, with their writing-brushes, they traced upon his breast and back, head and face and neck, limbs and hands and feet,—even upon the soles of his feet, and upon all parts of his body,—the text of the holy sûtra called *Hannya-Shin-Kyō*.* When this had been done, the priest instructed Hōichi, saying:—

* The Smaller Pragña-Pârmitâ-Hridaya-Sûtra is thus called in Japanese. Both the smaller and larger sûtras called Pragña-Pârmitâ ("Transcendent Wisdom") have been translated by the late Professor Max Müller, and can be found in volume xlix of the *Sacred*

"Tonight, as soon as I go away, you must seat yourself on the verandah, and wait. You will be called. But, whatever may happen, do not answer, and do not move. Say nothing and sit still—as if meditating. If you stir, or make any noise, you will be torn asunder. Do not get frightened; and do not think of calling for help—because no help could save you. If you do exactly as I tell you, the danger will pass, and you will have nothing more to fear."

After dark the priest and the acolyte went away; and Hōichi seated himself on the verandah, according to the instructions given him. He laid his biwa on the planking beside him, and, assuming the attitude of meditation, remained quite still,—taking care not to cough, or to breathe audibly. For hours he stayed thus.

Then, from the roadway, he heard the steps coming. They passed the gate, crossed the garden, approached the verandah, and stopped—directly in front of him.

"Hōichi!" the deep voice called. But the blind man held his breath, and sat motionless.

"Hōichi!" grimly called the voice a second time. Then a third time—savagely:—

"Hōichi!"

Hōichi remained as still as a stone,—and the voice grumbled:—

Books of the East ("Buddhist Mahâyâna Sûtras").—Apropos of the magical use of the text, as described in this story, it is worth remarking that the subject of the sûtra is the Doctrine of the Emptiness of Forms,—that is to say, of the unreal character of all phenomena or noumena. . . . "Form is emptiness; and emptiness is form. Emptiness is not different from form; form is not different from emptiness. What is form—that is emptiness. What is emptiness—that is form. . . . Perception, name, concept, and knowledge are also emptiness. . . . There is no eye, ear, nose, tongue, body, and mind. . . . But when the envelope of consciousness has been annihilated, and then he (the seeker) becomes free from all fear, and beyond the reach of change, enjoying final Nirvâna."

"No answer!—that won't do! . . . Must see where the fellow is. . . ."

There was a noise of heavy feet mounting upon the verandah. The feet approached deliberately,—halted beside him. Then, for long minutes,—during which Hōichi felt his whole body shake to the beating of his heart,—there was dead silence.

At last the gruff voice muttered close to him:—

"Here is the biwa; but of the biwa-player I see—only two ears! . . . So that explains why he did not answer: he had no mouth to answer with—there is nothing left of him but his ears. . . . Now to my lord those ears I will take—in proof that the august commands have been obeyed, so far as was possible. . . ."

At that instant Hōichi felt his ears gripped by fingers of iron, and torn off! Great as the pain was, he gave no cry. The heavy foot-falls receded along the verandah,—descended into the garden,— passed out to the roadway,—ceased. From either side of his head, the blind man felt a thick warm trickling; but he dared not lift his hands. . . .

Before sunrise the priest came back. He hastened at once to the verandah in the rear, stepped and slipped upon something clammy, and uttered a cry of horror;—for he saw, by the light of his lantern, that the clamminess was blood. But he perceived Hōichi sitting there, in the attitude of meditation—with the blood still oozing from his wounds.

"My poor Hōichi!" cried the startled priest,—"what is this? . . . You have been hurt?"

At the sound of his friend's voice, the blind man felt safe. He burst out sobbing, and tearfully told his adventure of the night.

"Poor, poor Hōichi!" the priest exclaimed,—"All my fault!—my very grievous fault! . . . Everywhere upon your body the holy texts had been written—except upon your ears! I trusted my acolyte to do that part of the work; and it was very, very wrong of me not to have made sure that he had done it! . . . Well, the matter cannot now be helped;—we can only try to heal your hurts as soon as possible. . . . Cheer up, friend!—the danger is now well over. You will never again be troubled by those visitors."

With the aid of a good doctor, Hōichi soon recovered from his injuries. The story of his strange adventure spread far and wide, and soon made him famous. Many noble persons went to Akamagaséki to hear him recite; and large presents of money were given to him,—so that he became a wealthy man. . . . But from the time of his adventure, he was known only by the appellation of *Mimi-nashi-Hōichi*: "Hōichi-the-Earless."

There was a falconer and hunter named Sonjō, who lived in the district called Tamura-no-Gō, of the province of Mutsu. One day he went out hunting, and could not find any game. But on his way home, at a place called Akanuma, he perceived a pair of *oshidori*** (mandarin-ducks), swimming together in a river that he was about to cross. To kill *oshidori* is not good; but Sonjō happened to be very hungry, and he shot at the pair. His arrow pierced the male: the female escaped into the rushes of the farther shore, and disappeared. Sonjō took the dead bird home, and cooked it.

That night he dreamed a dreary dream. It seemed to him that a beautiful woman came into his room, and stood by his pillow, and began to weep. So bitterly did she weep that Sonjō felt as if his heart were being torn out while he listened. And the woman cried to him: "Why,—oh! Why did you kill him?—of what wrong was he guilty? . . . At Akanuma we were so happy together,—and you killed him! . . . What harm did he ever do you? Do you even know what you have done?—oh! do you know what a cruel, what a wicked thing you have done? . . . Me too you have killed,—for I will not live without my husband! . . . Only to tell you this I came. . . ."
Then again she wept aloud,—so bitterly that the voice of her crying

---

* From ancient times, in the Far East, the birds have been regarded as emblems of conjugal affection.

pierced into the marrow of the listener's bones;—and she sobbed out the words of this poem:—

> *Hi kururéba*
> *Sasoëshi mono wo—*
> *Akanuma no*
> *Makomo no kuré no*
> *Hitori-né zo uki!*

(At the coming of twilight I invited him to return with me—! Now to sleep alone in the shadow of the rushes of Akanuma—ah! what misery unspeakable!)*

And after having uttered these verses she exclaimed:—"Ah, you do not know—you cannot know what you have done! But tomorrow, when you go to Akanuma, you will see,—you will see...." So saying, and weeping very piteously, she went away.

When Sonjō awoke in the morning, this dream remained so vivid in his mind that he was greatly troubled. He remembered the words:—"But tomorrow, when you go to Akanuma, you will see,—you will see." And he resolved to go there at once, that he might learn whether his dream was anything more than a dream.

So he went to Akanuma; and there, when he came to the river-bank, he saw the female *oshidori* swimming alone. In the same

---

* There is a pathetic double meaning in the third verse; for the syllables composing the proper name *Akanuma* ("Red Marsh") may also be read as *akanu-ma*, signifying "at the time of our inseparable (or delightful) relation." So the poem can also thus be rendered:—"When the day began to fail, I had invited him to accompany me ...! Now, after the time of that happy relation, what misery for the one who must slumber alone in the shadow of the rushes!"—The *makomo* is a sort of large rush, used for making baskets.

moment the bird perceived Sonjō; but, instead of trying to escape, she swam straight towards him, looking at him the while in a strange fixed way. Then, with her beak, she suddenly tore open her own body, and died before the hunter's eyes. . . .

Sonjō shaved his head, and became a priest.

A long time ago, in the town of Niigata, in the province of Echizen, there lived a man called Nagao Chōsei.

Nagao was the son of a physician, and was educated for his father's profession. At an early age he had been betrothed to a girl called O-Tei, the daughter of one of his father's friends; and both families had agreed that the wedding should take place as soon as Nagao had finished his studies. But the health of O-Tei proved to be weak; and in her fifteenth year she was attacked by a fatal consumption. When she became aware that she must die, she sent for Nagao to bid him farewell.

As he knelt at her bedside, she said to him:—

"Nagao-Sama, my betrothed, we were promised to each other from the time of our childhood; and we were to have been married at the end of this year. But now I am going to die;—the gods know what is best for us. If I were able to live for some years longer, I could only continue to be a cause of trouble and grief for others. With this frail body, I could not be a good wife; and therefore even to wish to live, for your sake, would be a very selfish wish. I am quite resigned to die; and I want you to promise that you will not grieve.... Besides, I want to tell you that I think we shall meet again...."

"Indeed we shall meet again," Nagao answered earnestly. "And in that Pure Land there will be no pain of separation."

"Nay, nay!" she responded softly, "I meant not the Pure Land. I believe that we are destined to meet again in this world,—although I shall be buried tomorrow."

Nagao looked at her wonderingly, and saw her smile at his wonder. She continued, in her gentle, dreamy voice,—

"Yes, I mean in this world,—in your own present life, Nagao-Sama.... Providing, indeed, that you wish it. Only, for this thing to happen, I must again be born a girl, and grow up to womanhood. So you would have to wait. Fifteen—sixteen years: that is a long time. . . . But, my promised husband, you are now only nineteen years old. . . ."

Eager to soothe her dying moments, he answered tenderly:—

"To wait for you, my betrothed, were no less a joy than a duty. We are pledged to each other for the time of seven existences."

"But you doubt?" she questioned, watching his face.

"My dear one," he answered, "I doubt whether I should be able to know you in another body, under another name,—unless you can tell me of a sign or token."

"That I cannot do," she said. "Only the Gods and the Buddhas know how and where we shall meet. But I am sure—very, very sure—that, if you be not unwilling to receive me, I shall be able to come back to you. . . . Remember these words of mine. . . ."

She ceased to speak; and her eyes closed. She was dead.

Nagao had been sincerely attached to O-Tei; and his grief was deep. He had a mortuary tablet made, inscribed with her *zokumyō*;* and

---

* The Buddhist term *zokumyō* ("profane name") signifies the personal name, borne during life, in contradiction to the *kaimyō* ("silâ-name") or *homyō* ("law-name") given after death,—religious posthumous appellations inscribed upon the tomb, and upon the

he placed the tablet in his *butsudan*,[*] and every day set offerings before it. He thought a great deal about the strange things that O-Tei had said to him just before her death; and, in the hope of pleasing her spirit, he wrote a solemn promise to wed her if she could ever return to him in another body. This written promise he sealed with his seal, and placed in the *butsudan* beside the mortuary tablet of O-Tei.

Nevertheless, as Nagao was an only son, it was necessary that he should marry. He soon found himself obliged to yield to the wishes of his family, and to accept a wife of his father's choosing. After his marriage he continued to set offerings before the tablet of O-Tei; and he never failed to remember her with affection. But by degrees her image became dim in his memory,—like a dream that is hard to recall. And the years went by.

During those years many misfortunes came upon him. He lost his parents by death,—then his wife and his only child. So that he found himself alone in the world. He abandoned his desolate home, and set out upon a long journey in the hope of forgetting his sorrows.

One day, in the course of his travels, he arrived at Ikao,—a mountain-village still famed for its thermal springs, and for the beautiful scenery of its neighborhood. In the village-inn at which he stopped, a young girl came to wait upon him; and, at the first sight of her face, he felt his heart leap as it had never leaped before. So strangely did she resemble O-Tei that he pinched himself to make sure that he was not dreaming. As she went and

mortuary tablet in the parish-temple.—For some account of these, see my paper titled "The Literature of the Dead" in *Exotics and Retrospectives*.

[*] Buddhist household shrine.

came,—bringing fire and food, or arranging the chamber of the guest,—her every attitude and motion revived in him some gracious memory of the girl to whom he had been pledged in his youth. He spoke to her; and she responded in a soft, clear voice of which the sweetness saddened him with a sadness of other days.

Then, in great wonder, he questioned her, saying:—

"Elder Sister, so much do you look like a person whom I knew long ago, that I was startled when you first entered this room. Pardon me, therefore, for asking what is your native place, and what is your name?"

Immediately,—and in the unforgotten voice of the dead,—she thus made answer:—

"My name is O-Tei; and you are Nagao Chōsei of Echigo, my promised husband. Seventeen years ago, I died in Niigata: then you made in writing a promise to marry me if ever I could come back to this world in the body of a woman;—and you sealed that written promise with your seal, and put it in the *butsudan*, beside the tablet inscribed with my name. And therefore I came back. . . ."

As she uttered these last words, she fell unconscious.

Nagao married her; and the marriage was a happy one. But at no time afterwards could she remember what she had told him in answer to his question at Ikao: neither could she remember anything of her previous existence. The recollection of the former birth,—mysteriously kindled in the moment of that meeting,— had again become obscured, and so thereafter remained.

Three hundred years ago, in the village called Asamimura, in the district called Onsengōri, in the province of Iyo, there lived a good man named Tokubei. This Tokubei was the richest person in the district, and the *muraosa*, or headman, of the village. In most matters he was fortunate; but he reached the age of forty without knowing the happiness of becoming a father. Therefore he and his wife, in the affliction of their childlessness, addressed many prayers to the divinity Fudō Myō Ō, who had a famous temple, called Saihōji, in Asamimura.

At last their prayers were heard: the wife of Tokubei gave birth to a daughter. The child was very pretty; and she received the name of Tsuyu. As the mother's milk was deficient, a milk-nurse, called O-Sodé, was hired for the little one.

O-Tsuyu grew up to be a very beautiful girl; but at the age of fifteen she fell sick, and the doctors thought that she was going to die. In that time the nurse O-Sodé, who loved O-Tsuyu with a real mother's love, went to the temple Saihōji, and fervently prayed to Fudō-Sama on behalf of the girl. Every day, for twenty-one days, she went to the temple and prayed; and at the end of that time, O-Tsuyu suddenly and completely recovered.

Then there was great rejoicing in the house of Tokubei; and he gave a feast to all his friends in celebration of the happy event. But on the night of the feast the nurse O-Sodé was suddenly taken ill; and on the following morning, the doctor, who had been summoned to attend her, announced that she was dying.

Then the family, in great sorrow, gathered about her bed, to bid her farewell. But she said to them:—

"It is time that I should tell you something which you do not know. My prayer has been heard. I besought Fudō-Sama that I might be permitted to die in the place of O-Tsuyu; and this great favor has been granted me. Therefore you must not grieve about my death. . . . But I have one request to make. I promised Fudō-Sama that I would have a cherry-tree planted in the garden of Saihōji, for a thank-offering and a commemoration. Now I shall not be able myself to plant the tree there: so I must beg that you will fulfill that vow for me. . . . Good-bye, dear friends; and remember that I was happy to die for O-Tsuyu's sake."

After the funeral of O-Sodé, a young cherry-tree,—the finest that could be found,—was planted in the garden of Saihōji by the parents of O-Tsuyu. The tree grew and flourished; and on the sixteenth day of the second month of the following year,— the anniversary of O-Sodé's death,—it blossomed in a wonderful way. So it continued to blossom for two hundred and fifty-four years,—always upon the sixteenth day of the second month;— and its flowers, pink and white, were like the nipples of a woman's breasts, bedewed with milk. And the people called it *Ubazakura*, the Cherry-tree of the Milk-Nurse.

It had been ordered that the execution should take place in the garden of the *yashiki*. So the man was taken there, and made to kneel down in a wide sanded space crossed by a line of *tobi-ishi*, or stepping-stones, such as you may still see in Japanese landscape-gardens. His arms were bound behind him. Retainers brought water in buckets, and rice-bags filled with pebbles; and they packed the rice-bags round the kneeling man,—so wedging him in that he could not move. The master came, and observed the arrangements. He found them satisfactory, and made no remarks.

Suddenly the condemned man cried out to him:—

"Honored Sir, the fault for which I have been doomed I did not wittingly commit. It was only my very great stupidity which caused the fault. Having been born stupid, by reason of my Karma, I could not always help making mistakes. But to kill a man for being stupid is wrong,—and that wrong will be repaid. So surely as you kill me, so surely shall I be avenged;—out of the resentment that you provoke will come the vengeance; and evil will be rendered for evil. . . ."

If any person be killed while feeling strong resentment, the ghost of that person will be able to take vengeance upon the killer. This the samurai knew. He replied very gently,—almost caressingly:—

"We shall allow you to frighten us as much as you please—after you are dead. But it is difficult to believe that you mean what you

say. Will you try to give us some sign of your great resentment—after your head has been cut off?"

"Assuredly I will," answered the man.

"Very well," said the samurai, drawing his long sword;—"I am now going to cut off your head. Directly in front of you there is a stepping-stone. After your head has been cut off, try to bite the stepping-stone. If your angry ghost can help you to do that, some of us may be frightened. . . . Will you try to bite the stone?"

"I will bite it!" cried the man, in great anger,—"I will bite it!—I will bite"—

There was a flash, a swish, a crunching thud: the bound body bowed over the rice sacks,—two long blood-jets pumping from the shorn neck;—and the head rolled upon the sand. Heavily toward the stepping-stone it rolled: then, suddenly bounding, it caught the upper edge of the stone between its teeth, clung desperately for a moment, and dropped inert.

None spoke; but the retainers stared in horror at their master. He seemed to be quite unconcerned. He merely held out his sword to the nearest attendant, who, with a wooden dipper, poured water over the blade from haft to point, and then carefully wiped the steel several times with sheets of soft paper. . . . And thus ended the ceremonial part of the incident.

For months thereafter, the retainers and the domestics lived in ceaseless fear of ghostly visitation. None of them doubted that the promised vengeance would come; and their constant terror caused them to hear and to see much that did not exist. They became afraid of the sound of the wind in the bamboos,—afraid even of the stirring of shadows in the garden. At last, after taking counsel together, they decided to petition their master to have a *Ségaki* service performed on behalf of the vengeful spirit.

"Quite unnecessary," the samurai said, when his chief retainer had uttered the general wish. . . . "I understand that the desire of a dying man for revenge may be a cause for fear. But in this case there is nothing to fear."

The retainer looked at his master beseechingly, but hesitated to ask the reason of the alarming confidence.

"Oh, the reason is simple enough," declared the samurai, divining the unspoken doubt. "Only the very last intention of the fellow could have been dangerous; and when I challenged him to give me the sign, I diverted his mind from the desire of revenge. He died with the set purpose of biting the stepping-stone; and that purpose he was able to accomplish, but nothing else. All the rest he must have forgotten. . . . So you need not feel any further anxiety about the matter."

—And indeed the dead man gave no more trouble. Nothing at all happened.

■ Of a Mirror and a Bell

Eight centuries ago, the priests of Mugenyama, in the province of Tōtōmi, wanted a big bell for their temple; and they asked the women of their parish to help them by contributing old bronze mirrors for bell-metal.

(Even today, in the courts of certain Japanese temples, you may see heaps of old bronze mirrors contributed for such a purpose. The largest collection of this kind that I ever saw was in the court of a temple of the Jōdo sect, at Hakata, in Kyūshū: the mirrors had been given for the making of a bronze statue of Amida, thirty-three feet high.)

There was at that time a young woman, a farmer's wife, living at Mugenyama, who presented her mirror to the temple, to be used for bell-metal. But afterwards she much regretted her mirror. She remembered things that her mother had told her about it; and she remembered that it had belonged not only to her mother but to her mother's mother and grandmother; and she remembered some happy smiles which it had reflected. Of course, if she could have offered the priests a certain sum of money in place of the mirror, she could have asked them to give back her heirloom. But she had not the money necessary. Whenever she went to the temple, she saw her mirror lying in the courtyard, behind a railing, among hundreds of other mirrors heaped there together. She knew it by the *Shō-Chiku-Bai* in relief on the back of it,—those three fortunate emblems of Pine, Bamboo, and Plumflower, which delighted her baby-eyes when her mother first showed her the mirror. She longed for some chance to steal the mirror, and hide it,—that she might thereafter treasure it always. But the chance did not come; and she became very unhappy,—and felt as if she had foolishly given away a part of her life. She thought about the old saying that a mirror is the Soul of a Woman—(a saying mystically expressed, by the Chinese character for Soul, engraved upon the backs of many bronze mirrors),—and she feared that it was true in weirder ways than she had before imagined. But she could not dare to speak of her pain to anybody.

Now, when all the mirrors contributed for the Mugenyama bell had been sent to the foundry, the bell-founders discovered that there was one mirror among them which would not melt. Again and again they tried to melt it; but it resisted all their efforts. Evidently the woman who had given that mirror to the temple must have regretted the giving. She had not presented her offering with all her heart; and therefore her selfish soul, remaining attached to the mirror, kept it hard and cold in the midst of the furnace.

Of course everybody heard of the matter, and everybody soon knew whose mirror it was that would not melt. And because of this public exposure of her secret fault, the poor woman became very much ashamed and very angry. And as she could not bear the shame, she drowned herself, after having written a farewell letter containing these words:—

When I am dead, it will not be difficult to melt the mirror and to cast the bell. But, to the person who breaks that bell by ringing it, great wealth will be given by the ghost of me.

—You must know that the last wish or promise of anybody who dies in anger, or performs suicide in anger, is generally supposed to possess a supernatural force. After the dead woman's mirror had been melted, and the bell had been successfully cast, people remembered the words of that letter. They felt sure that the spirit of the writer would give wealth to the breaker of the bell; and, as soon as the bell had been suspended in the court of the temple, they went in multitude to ring it. With all their might and main they swung the ringing-beam; but the bell proved to be a good bell, and it bravely withstood their assaults. Nevertheless, the people were not easily discouraged. Day after day, at all hours, they continued to ring the bell furiously,—caring nothing whatever for the protests of the priests. So the ringing became an affliction; and the priests could not endure it; and they got rid of the bell by rolling it down the hill into a swamp. The swamp was deep, and swallowed it up,— and that was the end of the bell. Only its legend remains; and in that legend it is called the *Mugen-Kané*, or Bell of Mugen.

Now there are queer old Japanese beliefs in the magical efficacy of a certain mental operation implied, though not described, by the verb *nazoraëru*. The word itself cannot be adequately rendered by any English word; for it is used in relation to many kinds of mimetic magic, as well as in relation to the performance of many religious acts of faith. Common meanings of *nazoraëru*, according to dictionaries, are "to imitate," "to compare," "to liken"; but the esoteric meaning is "to substitute, in imagination, one object or action for another, so as to bring about some magical or miraculous result."

For example:—you cannot afford to build a Buddhist temple; but you can easily lay a pebble before the image of the Buddha, with the same pious feeling that would prompt you to build a temple if you were rich enough to build one. The merit of so offering the pebble becomes equal, or almost equal, to the merit of erecting a temple. . . . You cannot read the six thousand seven hundred and seventy-one volumes of the Buddhist texts; but you can make a revolving library containing them turn round by pushing it like a windlass. And if you push with an earnest wish that you could read the six thousand seven hundred and seventy-one volumes, you will acquire the same merit as the reading of them would enable you to gain. . . . So much will perhaps suffice to explain the religious meanings of *nazoraëru*.

The magical meanings could not all be explained without a great variety of examples; but, for present purposes, the following will serve. If you should make a little man of straw, for the same reason that Sister Helen made a little man of wax,—and nail it, with nails not less than five inches long, to some tree in a temple-grove at the Hour of the Ox,—and if the person, imaginatively represented by that little straw man, should die thereafter in atrocious agony,— that would illustrate one signification of *nazoraëru*. . . . Or, let us suppose that a robber has entered your house during the night, and carried away your valuables. If you can discover the footprints of that robber in your garden, and then promptly burn a very large moxa on each of them, the soles of the feet of the robber will become inflamed, and will allow him no rest until he returns, of his own accord, to put himself at your mercy. That is another kind of mimetic magic expressed by the term *nazoraëru*. And a third kind is illustrated by various legends of the Mugen-Kané.

After the bell had been rolled into the swamp, there was, of course, no more chance of ringing it in such wise as to break it. But persons who regretted this loss of opportunity would strike and break objects imaginatively substituted for the bell,—thus hoping to please the spirit of the owner of the mirror that had made so much trouble. One of these persons was a woman called Umégaë,—famed in Japanese legend because of her relation to Kajiwara Kagésué, a warrior of the Heiké clan. While the pair were traveling together, Kajiwara one day found himself in great straits for want of money; and Umégaë, remembering the tradition of the Bell of Mugen, took a basin of bronze, and, mentally representing it to be the bell, beat upon it until she broke it,—crying out, at the same time, for three hundred pieces of gold. A guest of the inn where the pair were stopping made inquiry as to the cause of the banging and the crying, and, on learning the story of the trouble, actually presented Umégaë with three hundred *ryō* in gold. Afterwards a song was made about Umégaë's basin of bronze; and that song is sung by dancing girls even to this day:—

Umégaë no chōzubachi tataïté
O-kané ga déru naraba
Mina San mi-uké wo
Sōré tanomimasu

(If, by striking upon the wash-basin of Umégaë, I could
make honorable money come to me, then would I
negotiate for the freedom of all my girl-comrades.)

After this happening, the fame of the Mugen-Kané became great; and many people followed the example of Umégaë,—thereby hoping to emulate her luck. Among these folk was a dissolute farmer who lived near Mugenyama, on the bank of the Ōïgawa. Having wasted his substance in riotous living, this farmer made for himself, out of the mud in his garden, a clay-model of the Mugen-Kané; and he beat the clay-bell, and broke it,—crying out the while for great wealth.

Then, out of the ground before him, rose up the figure of a white-robed woman, with long loose-flowing hair, holding a covered jar. And the woman said: "I have come to answer your fervent prayer as it deserves to be answered. Take, therefore, this jar." So saying, she put the jar into his hands, and disappeared.

Into his house the happy man rushed, to tell his wife the good news. He set down in front of her the covered jar,—which was heavy,—and they opened it together. And they found that it was filled, up to the very brim, with. . . .

But no!—I really cannot tell you with what it was filled.

Once, when Musō Kokushi, a priest of the Zen sect, was journeying alone through the province of Mino, he lost his way in a mountain-district where there was nobody to direct him. For a long time he wandered about helplessly; and he was beginning to despair of finding shelter for the night, when he perceived, on the top of a hill lighted by the last rays of the sun, one of those little hermitages, called *anjitsu*, which are built for solitary priests. It seemed to be in ruinous condition; but he hastened to it eagerly, and found that it was inhabited by an aged priest, from whom he begged the favor of a night's lodging. This the old man harshly refused; but he directed Musō to a certain hamlet, in the valley adjoining, where lodging and food could be obtained.

Musō found his way to the hamlet, which consisted of less than a dozen farm-cottages; and he was kindly received at the dwelling of the headman. Forty or fifty persons were assembled in the principal apartment at the moment of Musō's arrival; but he was shown into a small separate room, where he was promptly supplied with food and bedding. Being very tired, he lay down to rest at an early hour; but a little before midnight he was roused from sleep by a sound of loud weeping in the next apartment. Presently the sliding-screens were gently pushed apart; and a young man, carrying a lighted lantern, entered the room, respectfully saluted him, and said:—

"Reverend Sir, it is my painful duty to tell you that I am now the responsible head of this house. Yesterday I was only the eldest son. But when you came here, tired as you were, we did not wish that you should feel embarrassed in any way: therefore we did not tell you that father had died only a few hours before. The people whom you saw in the next room are the inhabitants of this village: they all assembled here to pay their last respects to the dead; and now they are going to another village, about three miles off,—for by our custom, no one of us may remain in this village during the night after a death has taken place. We make the proper offerings and prayers;—then we go away, leaving the corpse alone. Strange things always happen in the house where a corpse has thus been left: so we think that it will be better for you to come away with us. We can find you good lodging in the other village. But perhaps, as you are a priest, you have no fear of demons or evil spirits; and, if you are not afraid of being left alone with the body, you will be very welcome to the use of this poor house. However, I must tell you that nobody, except a priest, would dare to remain here tonight."

Musō made answer:—

"For your kind intention and your generous hospitality, I am deeply grateful. But I am sorry that you did not tell me of your father's death when I came;—for, though I was a little tired, I certainly was not so tired that I should have found difficulty in doing my duty as a priest. Had you told me, I could have performed the service before your departure. As it is, I shall perform the service after you have gone away; and I shall stay by the body until morning. I do not know what you mean by your words about the danger of staying here alone; but I am not afraid of ghosts or demons: therefore please to feel no anxiety on my account."

The young man appeared to be rejoiced by these assurances, and expressed his gratitude in fitting words. Then the other members of the family, and the folk assembled in the adjoining room, having been told of the priest's kind promises, came to thank him,—after which the master of the house said:—

"Now, reverend Sir, much as we regret to leave you alone, we must bid you farewell. By the rule of our village, none of us can stay here after midnight. We beg, kind Sir, that you will take every care of your honorable body, while we are unable to attend upon you. And if you happen to hear or see anything strange during our absence, please tell us of the matter when we return in the morning."

All then left the house, except the priest, who went to the room where the dead body was lying. The usual offerings had been set before the corpse; and a small Buddhist lamp—*tōmyō*—was burning. The priest recited the service, and performed the funeral ceremonies,—after which he entered into meditation. So meditating he remained through several silent hours; and there was no sound in the deserted village. But, when the hush of the night was at its deepest, there noiselessly entered a Shape, vague and vast; and in the same moment Musō found himself without power to move or speak. He saw that Shape lift the corpse, as with hands, devour it, more quickly than a cat devours a rat,—beginning at the head, and eating everything: the hair and the bones and even the shroud. And the monstrous Thing, having thus consumed the body, turned to the offerings, and ate them also. Then it went away, as mysteriously as it had come.

When the villagers returned next morning, they found the priest awaiting them at the door of the headman's dwelling. All in turn saluted him; and when they had entered, and looked about the room, no one expressed any surprise at the disappearance of

the dead body and the offerings. But the master of the house said to Musō:—

"Reverend Sir, you have probably seen unpleasant things during the night: all of us were anxious about you. But now we are very happy to find you alive and unharmed. Gladly we would have stayed with you, if it had been possible. But the law of our village, as I told you last evening, obliges us to quit our houses after a death has taken place, and to leave the corpse alone. Whenever this law has been broken, heretofore, some great misfortune has followed. Whenever it is obeyed, we find that the corpse and the offerings disappear during our absence. Perhaps you have seen the cause."

Then Musō told of the dim and awful Shape that had entered the death-chamber to devour the body and the offerings. No person seemed to be surprised by his narration; and the master of the house observed:—

"What you have told us, reverend Sir, agrees with what has been said about this matter from ancient time."

Musō then inquired:—

"Does not the priest on the hill sometimes perform the funeral service for your dead?"

"What priest?" the young man asked.

"The priest who yesterday evening directed me to this village," answered Musō. "I called at his *anjitsu* on the hill yonder. He refused me lodging, but told me the way here."

The listeners looked at each other, as in astonishment; and, after a moment of silence, the master of the house said:—

"Reverend Sir, there is no priest and there is no *anjitsu* on the hill. For the time of many generations there has not been any resident-priest in this neighborhood."

Musō said nothing more on the subject; for it was evident that his kind hosts supposed him to have been deluded by some goblin. But after having bidden them farewell, and obtained all necessary information as to his road, he determined to look again for the hermitage on the hill, and so to ascertain whether he had really been deceived. He found the *anjitsu* without any difficulty; and, this time, its aged occupant invited him to enter. When he had done so, the hermit humbly bowed down before him, exclaiming:—"Ah! I am ashamed!—I am very much ashamed!—I am exceedingly ashamed!"

"You need not be ashamed for having refused me shelter," said Musō. "You directed me to the village yonder, where I was very kindly treated; and I thank you for that favor."

"I can give no man shelter," the recluse made answer; "—and it is not for the refusal that I am ashamed. I am ashamed only that you should have seen me in my real shape,—for it was I who devoured the corpse and the offerings last night before your eyes. . . . Know, reverend Sir, that I am a *jikininki*,*—an eater of human flesh. Have pity upon me, and suffer me to confess the secret fault by which I became reduced to this condition.

"A long, long time ago, I was a priest in this desolate region. There was no other priest for many leagues around. So, in that time, the bodies of the mountain-folk who died used to be brought here,—sometimes from great distances,—in order that I might repeat over them the holy service. But I repeated the service and

---

* Literally, a man-eating goblin. The Japanese narrator gives also the Sanskrit term, "Râkshasa"; but this word is quite as vague as *jikininki*, since there are many kinds of Râkshasas. Apparently the word *jikininki* signifies here one of the *Baramon-Rasetsu-Gaki*,—forming the twenty-sixth class of pretas enumerated in the old Buddhist books.

performed the rites only as a matter of business;—I thought only of the food and the clothes that my sacred profession enabled me to gain. And because of this selfish impiety I was reborn, immediately after my death, into the state of a jikininki. Since then I have been obliged to feed upon the corpses of the people who die in this district: every one of them I must devour in the way that you saw last night.... Now, reverend Sir, let me beseech you to perform a *Ségaki* service[*] for me: help me by your prayers, I entreat you, so that I may be soon able to escape from this horrible state of existence...."

No sooner had the hermit uttered this petition than he disappeared; and the hermitage also disappeared at the same instant. And Musō Kokushi found himself kneeling alone in the high grass, beside an ancient and moss-grown tomb of the form called *go-rin-ishi*,[†] which seemed to be the tomb of a priest.

[*] A *Ségaki* service is a special Buddhist service performed on behalf of beings supposed to have entered the condition of *gaki* (pretas), or hungry spirits. For a brief account of such a service, see my *Japanese Miscellany*.

[†] Literally, "five-circle (or five-zone) stone." A funeral monument consisting of five parts superimposed,—each of a different form,—symbolizing the five mystic elements: Ether, Air, Fire, Water, Earth.

On the Akasaka Road, in Tōkyō, there is a slope called Kii-no-kuni-zaka,—which means the Slope of the Province of Kii. I do not know why it is called the Slope of the Province of Kii. On one side of this slope you see an ancient moat, deep and very wide, with high green banks rising up to some place of gardens;—and on the other side of the road extend the long and lofty walls of an imperial palace. Before the era of street-lamps and jinrikishas, this neighborhood was very lonesome after dark; and belated pedestrians would go miles out of their way rather than mount the Kii-no-kuni-zaka, alone, after sunset.

All because of a Mujina that used to walk there.

The last man who saw the Mujina was an old merchant of the Kyōbashi quarter, who died about thirty years ago. This is the story, as he told it:—

One night, at a late hour, he was hurrying up the Kii-no-kuni-zaka, when he perceived a woman crouching by the moat, all alone, and weeping bitterly. Fearing that she intended to drown herself, he stopped to offer her any assistance or consolation in his power. She appeared to be a slight and graceful person, handsomely dressed; and her hair was arranged like that of a young

girl of good family. "O-jochū,"* he exclaimed, approaching her,—
"O-jochū, do not cry like that! . . . Tell me what the trouble is;
and if there be any way to help you, I shall be glad to help you."
(He really meant what he said; for he was a very kind man.) But
she continued to weep,—hiding her face from him with one of
her long sleeves. "O-jochū," he said again, as gently as he could,—
"please, please listen to me! . . . This is no place for a young lady
at night! Do not cry, I implore you!—only tell me how I may be
of some help to you!" Slowly she rose up, but turned her back to
him, and continued to moan and sob behind her sleeve. He laid
his hand lightly upon her shoulder, and pleaded:—"O-jochū!—
O-jochū!—O-jochū! . . . Listen to me, just for one little moment!
. . . O-jochū!—O-jochū! . . ." Then that O-jochū turned around,
and dropped her sleeve, and stroked her face with her hand;—
and the man saw that she had no eyes or nose or mouth,—and
he screamed and ran away.

Up Kii-no-kuni-zaka he ran and ran; and all was black and
empty before him. On and on he ran, never daring to look back;
and at last he saw a lantern, so far away that it looked like the gleam
of a firefly; and he made for it. It proved to be only the lantern of an
itinerant *soba*-seller,† who had set down his stand by the road-side;
but any light and any human companionship was good after that
experience; and he flung himself down at the feet of the soba-seller,
crying out, "Ah!—aa!!—aa!!! . . ."

"*Koré! koré!*" roughly exclaimed the soba-man. "Here! what is
the matter with you? Anybody hurt you?"

---

 * O-jochū ("honorable damsel"),—a polite form of address used in speaking to a
young lady whom one does not know.
 † *Soba* is a preparation of buckwheat, somewhat resembling vermicelli.

"No—nobody hurt me," panted the other,—"only . . . *Ah!—aa!*"

"—Only scared you?" queried the peddler, unsympathetically. "Robbers?"

"Not robbers,—not robbers," gasped the terrified man. . . . "I saw . . . I saw a woman—by the moat;—and she showed me. . . . *Ah!* I cannot tell you what she showed me! . . ."

"Hé! Was it anything like THIS that she showed you?" cried the soba-man, stroking his own face—which therewith became like unto an Egg. . . . And, simultaneously, the light went out.

Nearly five hundred years ago there was a samurai, named Isogai Héïdazaëmon Takétsura, in the service of the Lord Kikuji, of Kyūshū. This Isogai had inherited, from many warlike ancestors, a natural aptitude for military exercises, and extraordinary strength. While yet a boy he had surpassed his teachers in the art of swordsmanship, in archery, and in the use of the spear, and had displayed all the capacities of a daring and skillful soldier. Afterwards, in the time of the Eikyō* war, he so distinguished himself that high honors were bestowed upon him. But when the house of Kikuji came to ruin, Isogai found himself without a master. He might then easily have obtained service under another daimyō; but as he had never sought distinction for his own sake alone, and as his heart remained true to his former lord, he preferred to give up the world. So he cut off his hair, and became a traveling priest,—taking the Buddhist name of Kwairyō.

But always, under the *koromo*† of the priest, Kwairyō kept warm within him the heart of the samurai. As in other years he had laughed at peril, so now also he scorned danger; and in all weathers and all seasons he journeyed to preach the good Law in places where no other priest would have dared to go. For that age was an

---

* The period of Eikyō lasted from 1429–1441.
† The upper robe of a Buddhist priest is thus called.

age of violence and disorder; and upon the highways there was no security for the solitary traveler, even if he happened to be a priest.

In the course of his first long journey, Kwairyō had occasion to visit the province of Kai. One evening, as he was traveling through the mountains of that province, darkness overcame him in a very lonesome district, leagues away from any village. So he resigned himself to pass the night under the stars; and having found a suitable grassy spot, by the roadside, he lay down there, and prepared to sleep. He had always welcomed discomfort; and even a bare rock was for him a good bed, when nothing better could be found, and the root of a pine-tree an excellent pillow. His body was iron; and he never troubled himself about dews or rain or frost or snow.

Scarcely had he lain down when a man came along the road, carrying an axe and a great bundle of chopped wood. This woodcutter halted on seeing Kwairyō lying down, and, after a moment of silent observation, said to him in a tone of great surprise:—

"What kind of a man can you be, good Sir, that you dare to lie down alone in such a place as this? . . . There are haunters about here,—many of them. Are you not afraid of Hairy Things?"

"My friend," cheerfully answered Kwairyō, "I am only a wandering priest,—a 'Cloud-and-Water-Guest,' as folks call it: *Unsui-no-ryokaku*. And I am not in the least afraid of Hairy Things,—if you mean goblin-foxes, or goblin-badgers, or any creatures of that kind. As for lonesome places, I like them: they are suitable for meditation. I am accustomed to sleeping in the open air: and I have learned never to be anxious about my life."

"You must be indeed a brave man, Sir Priest," the peasant responded, "to lie down here! This place has a bad name,—a very bad name. But, as the proverb has it, *Kunshi ayayuki ni chikayorazu* ('The superior man does not needlessly expose himself to peril');

and I must assure you, Sir, that it is very dangerous to sleep here. Therefore, although my house is only a wretched thatched hut, let me beg of you to come home with me at once. In the way of food, I have nothing to offer you; but there is a roof at least, and you can sleep under it without risk."

He spoke earnestly; and Kwairyō, liking the kindly tone of the man, accepted this modest offer. The woodcutter guided him along a narrow path, leading up from the main road through mountain-forest. It was a rough and dangerous path,—sometimes skirting precipices,—sometimes offering nothing but a network of slippery roots for the foot to rest upon,—sometimes winding over or between masses of jagged rock. But at last Kwairyō found himself upon a cleared space at the top of a hill, with a full moon shining overhead; and he saw before him a small thatched cottage, cheerfully lighted from within. The woodcutter led him to a shed at the back of the house, whither water had been conducted, through bamboo-pipes, from some neighboring stream; and the two men washed their feet. Beyond the shed was a vegetable garden, and a grove of cedars and bamboos; and beyond the trees appeared the glimmer of a cascade, pouring from some loftier height, and swaying in the moonshine like a long white robe.

As Kwairyō entered the cottage with his guide, he perceived four persons—men and women—warming their hands at a little fire kindled in the *ro*[*] of the principal apartment. They bowed low to the priest, and greeted him in the most respectful manner. Kwairyō wondered that persons so poor, and dwelling in such a solitude,

---

[*] A sort of little fireplace, contrived in the floor of a room, is thus described. The *ro* is usually a square shallow cavity, lined with metal and half-filled with ashes, in which charcoal is lighted.

should be aware of the polite forms of greeting. "These are good people," he thought to himself; "and they must have been taught by some one well acquainted with the rules of propriety." Then turning to his host,—the *aruji*, or house-master, as the others called him,—Kwairyō said:—

"From the kindness of your speech, and from the very polite welcome given me by your household, I imagine that you have not always been a woodcutter. Perhaps you formerly belonged to one of the upper classes?"

Smiling, the woodcutter answered:—

"Sir, you are not mistaken. Though now living as you find me, I was once a person of some distinction. My story is the story of a ruined life—ruined by my own fault. I used to be in the service of a daimyō; and my rank in that service was not inconsiderable. But I loved women and wine too well; and under the influence of passion I acted wickedly. My selfishness brought about the ruin of our house, and caused the death of many persons. Retribution followed me; and I long remained a fugitive in the land. Now I often pray that I may be able to make some atonement for the evil which I did, and to reestablish the ancestral home. But I fear that I shall never find any way of so doing. Nevertheless, I try to overcome the karma of my errors by sincere repentance, and by helping as far as I can, those who are unfortunate."

Kwairyō was pleased by this announcement of good resolve; and he said to the aruji:—

"My friend, I have had occasion to observe that man, prone to folly in their youth, may in after years become very earnest in right living. In the holy sûtras it is written that those strongest in wrong-doing can become, by power of good resolve, the strongest in right-doing. I do not doubt that you have a good heart; and I hope that better fortune will come to you. Tonight I shall recite the sûtras for your sake, and pray that you may obtain the force to overcome the karma of any past errors."

With these assurances, Kwairyō bade the *aruji* good-night; and his host showed him to a very small side-room, where a bed had been made ready. Then all went to sleep except the priest, who began to read the sûtras by the light of a paper lantern. Until a late hour he continued to read and pray: then he opened a little window in his little sleeping-room, to take a last look at the landscape before lying down. The night was beautiful: there was no cloud in the sky; there was no wind; and the strong moonlight threw down sharp black shadows of foliage, and glittered on the dews of the garden. Shrillings of crickets and bell-insects made a musical tumult; and the sound of the neighboring cascade deepened with the night. Kwairyō felt thirsty as he listened to the noise of the water; and, remembering the bamboo aqueduct at the rear of the house, he thought that he could go there and get a drink without disturbing the sleeping household. Very gently he pushed apart the sliding-screens that separated his room from the main apartment; and he saw, by the light of the lantern, five recumbent bodies—without heads!

For one instant he stood bewildered,—imagining a crime. But in another moment he perceived that there was no blood, and that the headless necks did not look as if they had been cut. Then he thought to himself:—"Either this is an illusion made by goblins, or I have been lured into the dwelling of a Rokuro-Kubi.... In the book *Sōshinki* it is written that if one finds the body of a Rokuro-Kubi without its head, and removes the body to another place, the head will never be able to join itself again to the neck. And the book further says that when the head comes back and finds that its body has been moved, it will strike itself upon the floor three times,—bounding like a ball,—and will pant as in great fear, and presently die. Now, if these be Rokuro-Kubi, they mean me no good;—so I shall be justified in following the instructions of the book...."

He seized the body of the aruji by the feet, pulled it to the window, and pushed it out. Then he went to the back-door, which he found barred; and he surmised that the heads had made their exit through the smoke-hole in the roof, which had been left open. Gently unbarring the door, he made his way to the garden, and proceeded with all possible caution to the grove beyond it. He heard voices talking in the grove; and he went in the direction of the voices,—stealing from shadow to shadow, until he reached a good hiding-place. Then, from behind a trunk, he caught sight of the heads,—all five of them,—flitting about, and chatting as they flitted. They were eating worms and insects which they found on the ground or among the trees. Presently the head of the aruji stopped eating and said:—

"Ah, that traveling priest who came to-night!—how fat all his body is! When we shall have eaten him, our bellies will be well filled.... I was foolish to talk to him as I did;—it only set him to reciting the sûtras on behalf of my soul! To go near him while he is reciting would be difficult; and we cannot touch him so long as he is praying. But as it is now nearly morning, perhaps he has gone to sleep.... Some one of you go to the house and see what the fellow is doing."

Another head—the head of a young woman—immediately rose up and flitted to the house, lightly as a bat. After a few minutes it came back, and cried out huskily, in a tone of great alarm:—

"That traveling priest is not in the house;—he is gone! But that is not the worst of the matter. He has taken the body of our aruji; and I do not know where he has put it."

At this announcement the head of the aruji—distinctly visible in the moonlight—assumed a frightful aspect: its eyes opened monstrously; its hair stood up bristling; and its teeth gnashed. Then a cry burst from its lips; and—weeping tears of rage—it exclaimed:—

"Since my body has been moved, to rejoin it is not possible! Then I must die! . . . And all through the work of that priest! Before I die I will get at that priest!—I will tear him!—I will devour him! . . . *AND THERE HE IS*—behind that tree!—hiding behind that tree! See him!—the fat coward! . . ."

In the same moment, the head of the aruji, followed by the other four heads, sprang at Kwairyō. But the strong priest had already armed himself by plucking up a young tree; and with that tree he struck the heads as they came,—knocking them from him with tremendous blows. Four of them fled away. But the head of the aruji, though battered again and again, desperately continued to bound at the priest, and at last caught him by the left sleeve of his robe. Kwairyō, however, as quickly gripped the head by its topknot, and repeatedly struck it. It did not release its hold; but it uttered a long moan, and thereafter ceased to struggle. It was dead. But its teeth still held the sleeve; and, for all his great strength, Kwairyō could not force open the jaws.

With the head still hanging to his sleeve he went back to the house, and there caught sight of the other four Rokuro-Kubi squatting together, with their bruised and bleeding heads reunited to their bodies. But when they perceived him at the back-door all screamed, "The priest! the priest!"—and fled, through the other doorway, out into the woods.

Eastward the sky was brightening; day was about to dawn; and Kwairyō knew that the power of the goblins was limited to the hours of darkness. He looked at the head clinging to his sleeve,—its face all fouled with blood and foam and clay; and he laughed aloud as he thought to himself: "What a *miyagé!**—the head of a goblin!" After which he gathered together his few belongings, and leisurely descended the mountain to continue his journey.

Right on he journeyed, until he came to Suwa in Shinano; and into the main street of Suwa he solemnly strode, with the head dangling at his elbow. Then woman fainted, and children screamed and ran away; and there was a great crowding and clamoring until the *torité* (as the police in those days were called) seized the priest, and took him to jail. For they supposed the head to be the head of a murdered man who, in the moment of being killed, had caught the murderer's sleeve in his teeth. As for Kwairyō, he only smiled and said nothing when they questioned him. So, after having passed a night in prison, he was brought before the magistrates of the district. Then he was ordered to explain how he, a priest, had been found with the head of a man fastened to his sleeve, and why he had dared thus shamelessly to parade his crime in the sight of people.

Kwairyō laughed long and loudly at these questions; and then he said:—

"Sirs, I did not fasten the head to my sleeve: it fastened itself there—much against my will. And I have not committed any crime. For this is not the head of a man; it is the head of a goblin;—and, if I caused the death of the goblin, I did not do so by any shedding of blood, but simply by taking the precautions necessary to assure my own safety. . . ." And he proceeded to relate the whole of the

* A present made to friends or to the household on returning from a journey is thus called. Ordinarily, of course, the *miyagé* consists of something produced in the locality to which the journey has been made: this is the point of Kwairyō's jest.

adventure,—bursting into another hearty laugh as he told of his encounter with the five heads.

But the magistrates did not laugh. They judged him to be a hardened criminal, and his story an insult to their intelligence. Therefore, without further questioning, they decided to order his immediate execution,—all of them except one, a very old man. This aged officer had made no remark during the trial; but, after having heard the opinion of his colleagues, he rose up, and said:—

"Let us first examine the head carefully; for this, I think, has not yet been done. If the priest has spoken truth, the head itself should bear witness for him. . . . Bring the head here!"

So the head, still holding in its teeth the *koromo* that had been stripped from Kwairyō's shoulders, was put before the judges. The old man turned it round and round, carefully examined it, and discovered, on the nape of its neck, several strange red characters. He called the attention of his colleagues to these, and also bade them observe that the edges of the neck nowhere presented the appearance of having been cut by any weapon. On the contrary, the line of severance was smooth as the line at which a falling leaf detaches itself from the stem. . . . Then said the elder:—

"I am quite sure that the priest told us nothing but the truth. This is the head of a Rokuro-Kubi. In the book *Nan-hō-ī-butsu-shi* it is written that certain red characters can always be found upon the nape of the neck of a real Rokuro-Kubi. There are the characters: you can see for yourselves that they have not been painted. Moreover, it is well known that such goblins have been dwelling in the mountains of the province of Kai from very ancient time. . . . But you, Sir," he exclaimed, turning to Kwairyō,— "what sort of sturdy priest may you be? Certainly you have given proof of a courage that few priests possess; and you have the air of a soldier rather than a priest. Perhaps you once belonged to the samurai-class?"

"You have guessed rightly, Sir," Kwairyō responded. "Before becoming a priest, I long followed the profession of arms; and in those days I never feared man or devil. My name then was Isogai Héïdazaëmon Takétsura of Kyūshū: there may be some among you who remember it."

At the utterance of that name, a murmur of admiration filled the court-room; for there were many present who remembered it. And Kwairyō immediately found himself among friends instead of judges,—friends anxious to prove their admiration by fraternal kindness.

With honor they escorted him to the residence of the daimyō, who welcomed him, and feasted him, and made him a handsome present before allowing him to depart. When Kwairyō left Suwa, he was as happy as any priest is permitted to be in this transitory world. As for the head, he took it with him,—jocosely insisting that he intended it for a *miyagé*.

And now it only remains to tell what became of the head.

A day or two after leaving Suwa, Kwairyō met with a robber, who stopped him in a lonesome place, and bade him strip. Kwairyō at once removed his *koromo*, and offered it to the robber, who then first perceived what was hanging to the sleeve. Though brave, the highwayman was startled: he dropped the garment, and sprang back. Then he cried out:—"You!—what kind of a priest are you? Why, you are a worse man than I am! It is true that I have killed people; but I never walked about with anybody's head fastened to my sleeve. . . . Well, Sir priest, I suppose we are of the same calling; and I must say that I admire you! . . . Now that head would be of use to me: I could frighten people with it. Will you sell it? You can have my robe in exchange for your *koromo*; and I will give you five ryō for the head."

Kwairyō answered:—

"I shall let you have the head and the robe if you insist; but I must tell you that this is not the head of a man. It is a goblin's head. So, if you buy it, and have any trouble in consequence, please to remember that you were not deceived by me."

"What a nice priest you are!" exclaimed the robber. "You kill men, and jest about it! . . . But I am really in earnest. Here is my robe; and here is the money;—and let me have the head. . . . What is the use of joking?"

"Take the thing," said Kwairyō. "I was not joking. The only joke—if there be any joke at all—is that you are fool enough to pay good money for a goblin's head." And Kwairyō, loudly laughing, went upon his way.

Thus the robber got the head and the *koromo*; and for some time he played goblin-priest upon the highways. But, reaching the neighborhood of Suwa, he there learned the true story of the head; and he then became afraid that the spirit of the Rokuro-Kubi might give him trouble. So he made up his mind to take back the head to the place from which it had come, and to bury it with its body. He found his way to the lonely cottage in the mountains of Kai; but nobody was there, and he could not discover the body. Therefore he buried the head by itself, in the grove behind the cottage; and he had a tombstone set up over the grave; and he caused a *Ségaki* service to be performed on behalf of the spirit of the Rokuro-Kubi. And that tombstone—known as the Tombstone of the Rokuro-Kubi—may be seen (at least so the Japanese storyteller declares) even unto this day.

■ A Dead Secret

A long time ago, in the province of Tamba, there lived a rich merchant named Inamuraya Gensuké. He had a daughter called O-Sono. As she was very clever and pretty, he thought it would be a pity to let her grow up with only such teaching as the country-teachers could give her: so he sent her, in care of some trusty attendants, to Kyōto, that she might be trained in the polite accomplishments taught to the ladies of the capital. After she had thus been educated, she was married to a friend of her father's family—a merchant named Nagaraya;—and she lived happily with him for nearly four years. They had one child,—a boy. But O-Sono fell ill and died, in the fourth year after her marriage.

On the night after the funeral of O-Sono, her little son said that his mamma had come back, and was in the room upstairs. She had smiled at him, but would not talk to him: so he became afraid, and ran away. Then some of the family went upstairs to the room which had been O-Sono's; and they were startled to see, by the light of a small lamp which had been kindled before a shrine in that room, the figure of the dead mother. She appeared as if standing in front of a *tansu*, or chest of drawers, that still contained her ornaments and her wearing-apparel. Her head and shoulders could be very distinctly seen; but from the waist downwards the figure thinned into invisibility;—it was like an imperfect reflection of her, and transparent as a shadow on water.

Then the folk were afraid, and left the room. Below they consulted together; and the mother of O-Sono's husband said: "A woman is fond of her small things; and O-Sono was much attached to her belongings. Perhaps she has come back to look at them. Many dead persons will do that,—unless the things be given to the parish-temple. If we present O-Sono's robes and girdles to the temple, her spirit will probably find rest."

It was agreed that this should be done as soon as possible. So on the following morning the drawers were emptied; and all of O-Sono's ornaments and dresses were taken to the temple. But she came back the next night, and looked at the tansu as before. And she came back also on the night following, and the night after that, and every night;—and the house became a house of fear.

The mother of O-Sono's husband then went to the parish-temple, and told the chief priest all that had happened, and asked for ghostly counsel. The temple was a Zen temple; and the head-priest was a learned old man, known as Daigen Oshō. He said: "There must be something about which she is anxious, in or near that tansu."—"But we emptied all the drawers," replied the woman;—"there is nothing in the tansu."—"Well," said Daigen Oshō, "tonight I shall go to your house, and keep watch in that room, and see what can be done. You must give orders that no person shall enter the room while I am watching, unless I call."

After sundown, Daigen Oshō went to the house, and found the room made ready for him. He remained there alone, reading the sûtras; and nothing appeared until after the Hour of the

Rat.* Then the figure of O-Sono suddenly outlined itself in front of the tansu. Her face had a wistful look; and she kept her eyes fixed upon the tansu.

The priest uttered the holy formula prescribed in such cases, and then, addressing the figure by the *kaimyō*† of O-Sono, said:—"I have come here in order to help you. Perhaps in that tansu there is something about which you have reason to feel anxious. Shall I try to find it for you?" The shadow appeared to give assent by a slight motion of the head; and the priest, rising, opened the top drawer. It was empty. Successively he opened the second, the third, and the fourth drawer;—he searched carefully behind them and beneath them;—he carefully examined the interior of the chest. He found nothing. But the figure remained gazing as wistfully as before. "What can she want?" thought the priest. Suddenly it occurred to him that there might be something hidden under the paper with which the drawers were lined. He removed the lining of the first drawer:—nothing! He removed the lining of the second and third drawers:—still nothing. But under the lining of the lower-most drawer he found—a letter. "Is this the thing about which you have been troubled?" he asked. The shadow of the woman turned toward him,—her faint gaze fixed upon the letter. "Shall I burn it for you?" he asked. She bowed before him. "It shall be burned in the temple this very morning," he promised;—"and no one shall read it, except myself." The figure smiled and vanished.

* The Hour of the Rat (*Né-no-Koku*), according to the old Japanese method of reckoning time, was the first hour. It corresponded to the time between our midnight and two o'clock in the morning; for the ancient Japanese hours were each equal to two modern hours.

† *Kaimyō*, the posthumous Buddhist name, or religious name, given to the dead. Strictly speaking, the meaning of the word is silâ-name.

Dawn was breaking as the priest descended the stairs, to find the family waiting anxiously below. "Do not be anxious," he said to them: "She will not appear again." And she never did.

The letter was burned. It was a love-letter written to O-Sono in the time of her studies at Kyōto. But the priest alone knew what was in it; and the secret died with him.

In a village of Musashi Province, there lived two woodcutters: Mosaku and Minokichi. At the time of which I am speaking, Mosaku
was an old man; and Minokichi, his apprentice, was a lad of eighteen years. Every day they went together to a forest situated about
five miles from their village. On the way to that forest there is a
wide river to cross; and there is a ferry-boat. Several times a bridge
was built where the ferry is; but the bridge was each time carried
away by a flood. No common bridge can resist the current there
when the river rises.

Mosaku and Minokichi were on their way home, one very cold
evening, when a great snowstorm overtook them. They reached the
ferry; and they found that the boatman had gone away, leaving his
boat on the other side of the river. It was no day for swimming;
and the woodcutters took shelter in the ferryman's hut,—thinking
themselves lucky to find any shelter at all. There was no brazier
in the hut, nor any place in which to make a fire: it was only a
two-mat* hut, with a single door, but no window. Mosaku and
Minokichi fastened the door, and lay down to rest, with their straw
rain-coats over them. At first they did not feel very cold; and they
thought that the storm would soon be over.

---

* That is to say, with a floor-surface of about six feet square.

The old man almost immediately fell asleep; but the boy, Mino-kichi, lay awake a long time, listening to the awful wind, and the continual slashing of the snow against the door. The river was roaring; and the hut swayed and creaked like a junk at sea. It was a terrible storm; and the air was every moment becoming colder; and Minokichi shivered under his rain-coat. But at last, in spite of the cold, he too fell asleep.

He was awakened by a showering of snow in his face. The door of the hut had been forced open; and, by the snow-light (*yuki-akari*), he saw a woman in the room,—a woman all in white. She was bending above Mosaku, and blowing her breath upon him;— and her breath was like a bright white smoke. Almost in the same moment she turned to Minokichi, and stooped over him. He tried to cry out, but found that he could not utter any sound. The White Woman bent down over him, lower and lower, until her face almost touched him; and he saw that she was very beautiful,— though her eyes made him afraid. For a little time she continued to look at him;—then she smiled, and she whispered:—"I intended to treat you like the other man. But I cannot help feeling some pity for you,—because you are so young. . . . You are a pretty boy, Minokichi; and I will not hurt you now. But, if you ever tell anybody—even your own mother—about what you have seen this night, I shall know it; and then I will kill you. . . . Remember what I say!"

With these words, she turned from him, and passed through the doorway. Then he found himself able to move; and he sprang up, and looked out. But the woman was nowhere to be seen; and the snow was driving furiously into the hut. Minokichi closed the door, and secured it by fixing several billets of wood against it. He wondered if the wind had blown it open;—he thought that he might have been only dreaming, and might have mistaken the gleam of the snow-light in the doorway for the figure of a white woman: but he could not be sure. He called to Mosaku, and was frightened because the old man did not answer. He put out his hand in the dark, and touched Mosaku's face, and found that it was ice! Mosaku was stark and dead. . . .

By dawn the storm was over; and when the ferryman returned to his station, a little after sunrise, he found Minokichi lying senseless beside the frozen body of Mosaku. Minokichi was promptly cared for, and soon came to himself; but he remained a long time ill from the effects of the cold of that terrible night. He had been greatly frightened also by the old man's death; but he said nothing about the vision of the woman in white. As soon as he got well again, he returned to his calling,—going alone every morning to the forest, and coming back at nightfall with his bundles of wood, which his mother helped him to sell.

One evening, in the winter of the following year, as he was on his way home, he overtook a girl who happened to be traveling by the same road. She was a tall, slim girl, very good-looking; and she answered Minokichi's greeting in a voice as pleasant to the ear as the voice of a song-bird. Then he walked beside her; and they began to talk. The girl said that her name was O-Yuki;[*] that she had lately lost both of her parents; and that she was going to Yedo, where she happened to have some poor relations, who might help her to find a situation as a servant. Minokichi soon felt charmed by this strange girl; and the more that he looked at her, the handsomer she appeared to be. He asked her whether she was yet betrothed;

---

[*] This name, signifying "Snow," is not uncommon. On the subject of Japanese female names, see my paper in the volume titled *Shadowings*.

and she answered, laughingly, that she was free. Then, in her turn, she asked Minokichi whether he was married, or pledged to marry; and he told her that, although he had only a widowed mother to support, the question of an "honorable daughter-in-law" had not yet been considered, as he was very young. . . . After these confidences, they walked on for a long while without speaking; but, as the proverb declares, *Ki ga aréba, mé mo kuchi hodo ni mono wo iu:* "When the wish is there, the eyes can say as much as the mouth." By the time they reached the village, they had become very much pleased with each other; and then Minokichi asked O-Yuki to rest awhile at his house. After some shy hesitation, she went there with him; and his mother made her welcome, and prepared a warm meal for her. O-Yuki behaved so nicely that Minokichi's mother took a sudden fancy to her, and persuaded her to delay her journey to Yedo. And the natural end of the matter was that Yuki never went to Yedo at all. She remained in the house, as an "honorable daughter-in-law."

O-Yuki proved a very good daughter-in-law. When Minokichi's mother came to die,—some five years later,—her last words were words of affection and praise for the wife of her son. And O-Yuki bore Minokichi ten children, boys and girls,—handsome children all of them, and very fair of skin.

The country-folk thought O-Yuki a wonderful person, by nature different from themselves. Most of the peasant-women age early; but O-Yuki, even after having become the mother of ten children, looked as young and fresh as on the day when she had first come to the village.

One night, after the children had gone to sleep, O-Yuki was sewing by the light of a paper lamp; and Minokichi, watching her, said:—

"To see you sewing there, with the light on your face, makes me think of a strange thing that happened when I was a lad of eighteen. I then saw somebody as beautiful and white as you are now—indeed, she was very like you. . . ."

Without lifting her eyes from her work, O-Yuki responded:—

"Tell me about her. . . . Where did you see her?"

Then Minokichi told her about the terrible night in the ferry-man's hut,—and about the White Woman that had stooped above him, smiling and whispering,—and about the silent death of old Mosaku. And he said:—

"Asleep or awake, that was the only time that I saw a being as beautiful as you. Of course, she was not a human being; and I was afraid of her,—very much afraid,—but she was so white! . . . Indeed, I have never been sure whether it was a dream that I saw, or the Woman of the Snow. . . ."

O-Yuki flung down her sewing, and arose, and bowed above Minokichi where he sat, and shrieked into his face:—

"It was I—I—I! Yuki it was! And I told you then that I would kill you if you ever said one word about it! . . . But for those children asleep there, I would kill you this moment! And now you had better take very, very good care of them; for if ever they have reason to complain of you, I will treat you as you deserve! . . ."

Even as she screamed, her voice became thin, like a crying of wind;—then she melted into a bright white mist that spired to the roof-beams, and shuddered away through the smoke-hold. . . . Never again was she seen.

In the era of Bummei (1469–1486) there was a young samurai called Tomotada in the service of Hatakéyama Yoshimuné, the Lord of Noto. Tomotada was a native of Echizen; but at an early age he had been taken, as page, into the palace of the daimyō of Noto, and had been educated, under the supervision of that prince, for the profession of arms. As he grew up, he proved himself both a good scholar and a good soldier, and continued to enjoy the favor of his prince. Being gifted with an amiable character, a winning address, and a very handsome person, he was admired and much liked by his samurai-comrades.

When Tomotada was about twenty years old, he was sent upon a private mission to Hosokawa Masamoto, the great daimyō of Kyōto, a kinsman of Hatakéyama Yoshimuné. Having been ordered to journey through Echizen, the youth requested and obtained permission to pay a visit, on the way, to his widowed mother.

It was the coldest period of the year when he started; and, though mounted upon a powerful horse, he found himself obliged to proceed slowly. The road which he followed passed through a mountain-district where the settlements were few and far between; and on the second day of his journey, after a weary ride of hours, he was dismayed to find that he could not reach his intended halting-place until late in the night. He had reason to be anxious;—for a

heavy snowstorm came on, with an intensely cold wind; and the horse showed signs of exhaustion. But in that trying moment, Tomotada unexpectedly perceived the thatched room of a cottage on the summit of a near hill, where willow-trees were growing. With difficulty he urged his tired animal to the dwelling; and he loudly knocked upon the storm-doors, which had been closed against the wind. An old woman opened them, and cried out compassionately at the sight of the handsome stranger: "Ah, how pitiful!—a young gentleman traveling alone in such weather! . . . Deign, young master, to enter."

Tomotada dismounted, and after leading his horse to a shed in the rear, entered the cottage, where he saw an old man and a girl warming themselves by a fire of bamboo splints. They respectfully invited him to approach the fire; and the old folks then proceeded to warm some rice-wine, and to prepare food for the traveler, whom they ventured to question in regard to his journey. Meanwhile the young girl disappeared behind a screen. Tomotada had observed, with astonishment, that she was extremely beautiful,—though her attire was of the most wretched kind, and her long, loose hair in disorder. He wondered that so handsome a girl should be living in such a miserable and lonesome place.

The old man said to him:—

"Honored Sir, the next village is far; and the snow is falling thickly. The wind is piercing; and the road is very bad. Therefore, to proceed further this night would probably be dangerous. Although this hovel is unworthy of your presence, and although we have not any comfort to offer, perhaps it were safer to remain tonight under this miserable roof. . . . We would take good care of your horse."

Tomotada accepted this humble proposal,—secretly glad of the chance thus afforded him to see more of the young girl. Presently a coarse but ample meal was set before him; and the girl came from behind the screen, to serve the wine. She was now reclad, in a rough but cleanly robe of homespun; and her long, loose hair had been neatly combed and smoothed. As she bent forward to fill his cup, Tomotada was amazed to perceive that she was incomparably more beautiful than any woman whom he had ever before seen; and there was a grace about her every motion that astonished him. But the elders began to apologize for her, saying: "Sir, our daughter, Aoyagi,* has been brought up here in the mountains, almost alone; and she knows nothing of gentle service. We pray that you will pardon her stupidity and her ignorance." Tomotada protested that he deemed himself lucky to be waited upon by so comely a maiden. He could not turn his eyes away from her—though he saw that his admiring gaze made her blush;—and he left the wine and food untasted before him. The mother said: "Kind Sir, we very much hope that you will try to eat and to drink a little,—though our peasant-fare is of the worst,—as you must have been chilled by that piercing wind." Then, to please the old folks, Tomotada ate and drank as he could; but the charm of the blushing girl still grew upon him. He talked with her, and found that her speech was sweet as her face. Brought up in the mountains as she might have been;—but, in that case, her parents must at some time been persons of high degree; for she spoke and moved like a damsel of rank. Suddenly he addressed her with a poem—which was also a question—inspired by the delight in his heart:—

* The name signifies "Green Willow";—though rarely met with, it is still in use.

"Tadzunétsuru,
Hana ka toté koso,
Hi wo kurasé,
Akénu ni otoru
Akané sasuran?"

("Being on my way to pay a visit, I found that which
I took to be a flower: therefore here I spend the day. . . .
Why, in the time before dawn, the dawn-blush tint
should glow—that, indeed, I know not.")*

Without a moment's hesitation, she answered him in these
verses:—

"Izuru hi no
Honoméku iro wo
Waga sodé ni
Tsutsumaba asu mo
Kimiya tomaran."

("If with my sleeve I hid the faint fair color of the dawning
sun,—then, perhaps, in the morning my lord will remain.")†

---

* The poem may be read in two ways; several of the phrases have a double meaning.
But the art of its construction would need considerable space to explain, and could scarcely
interest the Western reader. The meaning that Tomotada desired to convey might be thus
expressed:—"While journeying to visit my mother, I met with a being lovely as a flower;
and for the sake of that lovely person, I am passing the day here. . . . Fair one, wherefore that
dawn-like blush before the hour of dawn?—can it mean that you love me?"

† Another reading is possible; but this one gives the signification of the *answer*
intended.

Then Tomotada knew that she accepted his admiration; and he was scarcely less surprised by the art with which she had uttered her feelings in verse, than delighted by the assurance which the verses conveyed. He was now certain that in all this world he could not hope to meet, much less to win, a girl more beautiful and witty than this rustic maid before him; and a voice in his heart seemed to cry out urgently, "Take the luck that the gods have put in your way!" In short he was bewitched—bewitched to such a degree that, without further preliminary, he asked the old people to give him their daughter in marriage,—telling them, at the same time, his name and lineage, and his rank in the train of the Lord of Noto.

They bowed down before him, with many exclamations of grateful astonishment. But, after some moments of apparent hesitation, the father replied:—

"Honored master, you are a person of high position, and likely to rise to still higher things. Too great is the favor that you deign to offer us;—indeed, the depth of our gratitude therefore is not to be spoken or measured. But this girl of ours, being a stupid country-girl of vulgar birth, with no training or teaching of any sort, it would be improper to let her become the wife of a noble samurai. Even to speak of such a matter is not right. . . . But, since you find the girl to your liking, and have condescended to pardon her peasant-manners and to overlook her great rudeness, we do gladly present her to you, for a humble handmaid. Deign, therefore, to act hereafter in her regard according to your august pleasure."

Ere morning the storm had passed; and day broke through a cloudless east. Even if the sleeve of Aoyagi hid from her lover's eyes the rose-blush of that dawn, he could no longer tarry. But neither could he resign himself to part with the girl; and, when everything had been prepared for his journey, he thus addressed her parents:—

"Though it may seem thankless to ask for more than I have already received, I must again beg you to give me your daughter for my wife. It would be difficult for me to separate from her now; and as she is willing to accompany me, if you permit, I can take her with me as she is. If you will give her to me, I shall ever cherish you as parents. . . . And, in the meantime, please to accept this poor acknowledgment of your kindest hospitality."

So saying, he placed before his humble host a purse of gold *ryō*. But the old man, after many prostrations, gently pushed back the gift, and said:—

"Kind master, the gold would be of no use to us; and you will probably have need of it during your long, cold journey. Here we buy nothing; and we could not spend so much money upon ourselves, even if we wished. . . . As for the girl, we have already bestowed her as a free gift;—she belongs to you: therefore it is not necessary to ask our leave to take her away. Already she has told us that she hopes to accompany you, and to remain your servant for as long as you may be willing to endure her presence. We are only too happy to know that you deign to accept her; and we pray that you will not trouble yourself on our account. In this place we could not provide her with proper clothing,—much less with a dowry. Moreover, being old, we should in any event have to separate from her before long. Therefore it is very fortunate that you should be willing to take her with you now."

It was in vain that Tomotada tried to persuade the old people to accept a present: he found that they cared nothing for money. But he saw that they were really anxious to trust their daughter's fate to his hands; and he therefore decided to take her with him. So he placed her upon his horse, and bade the old folks farewell for the time being, with many sincere expressions of gratitude.

"Honored Sir," the father made answer, "it is we, and not you, who have reason for gratitude. We are sure that you will be kind to our girl; and we have no fears for her sake. . . ."

(Here, in the Japanese original, there is a queer break in the natural course of the narration, which therefrom remains curiously inconsistent. Nothing further is said about the mother of Tomotada, or about the parents of Aoyagi, or about the daimyō of Noto. Evidently the writer wearied of his work at this point, and hurried the story, very carelessly, to its startling end. I am not able to supply his omissions, or to repair his faults of construction; but I must venture to put in a few explanatory details, without which the rest of the tale would not hold together. . . . It appears that Tomotada rashly took Aoyagi with him to Kyōto, and so got into trouble; but we are not informed as to where the couple lived afterwards.)

. . . Now a samurai was not allowed to marry without the consent of his lord; and Tomotada could not expect to obtain this sanction before his mission had been accomplished. He had reason, under such circumstances, to fear that the beauty of Aoyagi might attract dangerous attention, and that means might be devised of taking her away from him. In Kyōto he therefore tried to keep her hidden from curious eyes. But a retainer of Lord Hosokawa one day caught sight of Aoyagi, discovered her relation to Tomotada, and reported the matter to the daimyō. Thereupon the daimyō—a young prince, and fond of pretty faces—gave orders that the girl should be brought to the palace; and she was taken thither at once, without ceremony.

Tomotada sorrowed unspeakably; but he knew himself powerless. He was only a humble messenger in the service of a far-off daimyō; and for the time being he was at the mercy of a much more powerful daimyō, whose wishes were not to be questioned. Moreover Tomotada knew that he had acted foolishly,—that he had brought about his own misfortune, by entering into a clandestine relation which the code of the military class condemned. There was now but one hope for him,—a desperate hope: that Aoyagi might be able and willing to escape and to flee with him. After long reflection, he resolved to try to send her a letter. The attempt would be dangerous, of course: any writing sent to her might find its way to the hands of the daimyō; and to send a love-letter to any inmate of the palace was an unpardonable offense. But he resolved to dare the risk; and, in the form of a Chinese poem, he composed a letter which he endeavored to have conveyed to her. The poem was written with only twenty-eight characters. But with those twenty-eight characters he was about to express all the depth of his passion, and to suggest all the pain of his loss:—*

> *Kōshi ō-son gojin wo ou;*
> *Ryokuju namida wo tarété rakin wo hitataru;*
> *Komon hitotabi irité fukaki koto umi no gotoshi;*
> *Koré yori shorō koré rojin.*

(Closely, closely the youthful prince now
follows after the gem-bright maid;—
The tears of the fair one, falling,
have moistened all her robes.

---

* So the Japanese storyteller would have us believe,—although the verses seem commonplace in translation. I have tried to give only their general meaning: an effective literal translation would require some scholarship.

But the august lord, having once become
enamored of her—the depth of his longing
is like the depth of the sea.
Therefore it is only I that am left forlorn,—
only I that am left to wander alone.)

On the evening of the day after this poem had been sent, Tomotada was summoned to appear before the Lord Hosokawa. The
youth at once suspected that his confidence had been betrayed; and
he could not hope, if his letter had been seen by the daimyō, to
escape the severest penalty. "Now he will order my death," thought
Tomotada;—"but I do not care to live unless Aoyagi be restored
to me. Besides, if the death-sentence be passed, I can at least try to
kill Hosokawa." He slipped his swords into his girdle, and hastened
to the palace.

On entering the presence-room he saw the Lord Hosokawa
seated upon the dais, surrounded by samurai of high rank, in
caps and robes of ceremony. All were silent as statues; and while
Tomotada advanced to make obeisance, the hush seemed to him
sinister and heavy, like the stillness before a storm. But Hosokawa
suddenly descended from the dais, and, while taking the youth by
the arm, began to repeat the words of the poem:—"*Kōshi ō-son
gojin wo ou. . . .*" And Tomotada, looking up, saw kindly tears in
the prince's eyes.

Then said Hosokawa:—

"Because you love each other so much, I have taken it upon
myself to authorize your marriage, in lieu of my kinsman, the Lord
of Noto; and your wedding shall now be celebrated before me. The
guests are assembled;—the gifts are ready."

At a signal from the lord, the sliding-screens concealing a further apartment were pushed open; and Tomotada saw there many dignitaries of the court, assembled for the ceremony, and Aoyagi awaiting him in bride's apparel. . . . Thus was she given back to him;—and the wedding was joyous and splendid;—and precious gifts were made to the young couple by the prince, and by the members of his household.

For five happy years, after that wedding, Tomotada and Aoyagi dwelt together. But one morning Aoyagi, while talking with her husband about some household matter, suddenly uttered a great cry of pain, and then became very white and still. After a few moments she said, in a feeble voice: "Pardon me for thus rudely crying out—but the pain was so sudden! . . . My dear husband, our union must have been brought about through some karma-relation in a former state of existence; and that happy relation, I think, will bring us again together in more than one life to come. But for this present existence of ours, the relation is now ended;—we are about to be separated. Repeat for me, I beseech you, the *Nembutsu*-prayer,—because I am dying."

"Oh! what strange wild fancies!" cried the startled husband,—"you are only a little unwell, my dear one! . . . lie down for a while, and rest; and the sickness will pass. . . ."

"No, no!" she responded—"I am dying!—I do not imagine it;—I know! . . . And it were needless now, my dear husband, to hide the truth from you any longer:—I am not a human being. The soul of a tree is my soul;—the heart of a tree is my heart;—the sap of the willow is my life. And some one, at this cruel moment, is cutting down my tree;—that is why I must die! . . . Even to weep were now beyond my strength!—quickly, quickly repeat the *Nembutsu* for me . . . quickly! . . . Ah! . . ."

With another cry of pain she turned aside her beautiful head, and tried to hide her face behind her sleeve. But almost in the same moment her whole form appeared to collapse in the strangest way, and to sink down, down, down—level with the floor. Tomotada had sprung to support her;—but there was nothing to support! There lay on the matting only the empty robes of the fair creature and the ornaments that she had worn in her hair: the body had ceased to exist. . . .

Tomotada shaved his head, took the Buddhist vows, and became an itinerant priest. He traveled through all the provinces of the empire; and, at holy places which he visited, he offered up prayers for the soul of Aoyagi. Reaching Echizen, in the course of his pilgrimage, he sought the home of the parents of his beloved. But when he arrived at the lonely place among the hills, where their dwelling had been, he found that the cottage had disappeared. There was nothing to mark even the spot where it had stood, except the stumps of three willows—two old trees and one young tree—that had been cut down long before his arrival.

Beside the stumps of those willow-trees he erected a memorial tomb, inscribed with diverse holy texts; and he there performed many Buddhist services on behalf of the spirits of Aoyagi and of her parents.

In Wakégōri, a district of the province of Iyo, there is a very ancient and famous cherry-tree, called *Jiu-roku-zakura*, or "the Cherry-tree of the Sixteenth Day," because it blooms every year upon the sixteenth day of the first month (by the old lunar calendar),—and only upon that day. Thus the time of its flowering is the Period of Great Cold,—though the natural habit of a cherry-tree is to wait for the spring season before venturing to blossom. But the Jiu-roku-zakura blossoms with a life that is not—or, at least, that was not originally—its own. There is the ghost of a man in that tree.

He was a samurai of Iyo; and the tree grew in his garden; and it used to flower at the usual time,—that is to say, about the end of March or the beginning of April. He had played under that tree when he was a child; and his parents and grandparents and ancestors had hung on its blossoming branches, season after season for more than a hundred years, bright strips of colored paper inscribed with poems of praise. He himself became very old,—outliving all his children; and there was nothing in the world left for him to live for except that tree. And lo! In the summer of a certain year, the tree withered and died!

Exceedingly the old man sorrowed for his tree. Then kind neighbors found for him a young and beautiful cherry-tree, and planted it in his garden,—hoping thus to comfort him. And he thanked them, and pretended to be glad. But really his heart was full of pain; for he had loved the old tree so well that nothing could have consoled him for the loss of it.

At last there came to him a happy thought: he remembered a way by which the perishing tree might be saved. (It was the sixteenth day of the first month.) Along he went into his garden, and bowed down before the withered tree, and spoke to it, saying: "Now deign, I beseech you, once more to bloom,—because I am going to die in your stead." (For it is believed that one can really give away one's life to another person, or to a creature or even to a tree, by the favor of the gods;—and thus to transfer one's life is expressed by the term *migawari ni tatsu,* "to act as a substitute.") Then under that tree he spread a white cloth, and diverse coverings, and sat down upon the coverings, and performed *hara-kiri* after the fashion of a samurai. And the ghost of him went into the tree, and made it blossom in that same hour.

And every year it still blooms on the sixteenth day of the first month, in the season of snow.

■ The Dream of Akinosuké

In the district called Toïchi of Yamato Province, there used to live a gōshi named Miyata Akinosuké. . . . (Here I must tell you that in Japanese feudal times there was a privileged class of soldier-farmers,—free-holders,—corresponding to the class of yeomen in England; and these were called gōshi.)

In Akinosuké's garden there was a great and ancient cedar-tree, under which he was wont to rest on sultry days. One very warm afternoon he was sitting under this tree with two of his friends, fellow-gōshi, chatting and drinking wine, when he felt all of a sudden very drowsy,—so drowsy that he begged his friends to excuse him for taking a nap in their presence. Then he lay down at the foot of the tree, and dreamed this dream:—

He thought that as he was lying there in his garden, he saw a procession, like the train of some great daimyō descending a hill nearby, and that he got up to look at it. A very grand procession it proved to be,—more imposing than anything of the kind which he had ever seen before; and it was advancing toward his dwelling. He observed in the van of it a number of young men richly appareled, who were drawing a great lacquered palace-carriage, or *gosho-guruma*, hung with bright blue silk. When the procession arrived within a short distance of the house it halted; and a richly dressed man—evidently a person of rank—advanced from it, approached Akinosuké, bowed to him profoundly, and then said:—

185

"Honored Sir, you see before you a *kérai* (vassal) of the Kokuō of Tokoyo.* My master, the King, commands me to greet you in his august name, and to place myself wholly at your disposal. He also bids me inform you that he augustly desires your presence at the palace. Be therefore pleased immediately to enter this honorable carriage, which he has sent for your conveyance."

Upon hearing these words Akinosuké wanted to make some fitting reply; but he was too much astonished and embarrassed for speech;—and in the same moment his will seemed to melt away from him, so that he could only do as the kérai bade him. He entered the carriage; the kérai took a place beside him, and made a signal; the drawers, seizing the silken ropes, turned the great vehicle southward;—and the journey began.

In a very short time, to Akinosuké's amazement, the carriage stopped in front of a huge two-storied gateway (*rōmon*), of a Chinese style, which he had never before seen. Here the kérai dismounted, saying, "I go to announce the honorable arrival,"—and he disappeared. After some little waiting, Akinosuké saw two noble-looking men, wearing robes of purple silk and high caps of the form indicating lofty rank, come from the gateway. These, after having respectfully saluted him, helped him to descend from the carriage, and led him through the great gate and across a vast garden, to the entrance of a palace whose front appeared to extend, west and east, to a distance of miles. Akinosuké was then shown into a reception-room of wonderful size and splendor. His guides conducted him

---

* The name of "Tokoyo" is indefinite. According to circumstances it may signify any unknown country,—or that undiscovered country from whose bourn no traveler returns,—or that Fairyland of far-eastern fable, the Realm of Hōrai. The term "Kokuō" means the ruler of the country,—therefore a king. The original phrase, *Tokoyo no Kukuō*, might be rendered here as "the Ruler of Hōrai," or "the King of Fairyland."

to the place of honor, and respectfully seated themselves apart; while serving-maids, in costume of ceremony, brought refreshments. When Akinosuké had partaken of the refreshments, the two purple-robed attendants bowed low before him, and addressed him in the following words,—each speaking alternately, according to the etiquette of courts:—

"It is now our honorable duty to inform you . . . as to the reason of your having been summoned hither. . . . Our master, the King, augustly desires that you become his son-in-law; . . . and it is his wish and command that you shall wed this very day . . . the August Princess, his maiden-daughter. . . . We shall soon conduct you to the presence-chamber . . . where His Augustness even now is waiting to receive you. . . . But it will be necessary that we first invest you . . . with the appropriate garments of ceremony."*

Having thus spoken, the attendants rose together, and proceeded to an alcove containing a great chest of gold lacquer. They opened the chest, and took from it various robes and girdles of rich material, and a *kamuri*, or regal headdress. With these they attired Akinosuké as befitted a princely bridegroom; and he was then conducted to the presence-room, where he saw the Kokuō of Tokoyo seated upon the *daiza*,† wearing a high black cap of state, and robed in yellow silk. Before the daiza, to left and right, a multitude of dignitaries sat in rank, motionless and splendid as images in a temple; and Akinosuké, advancing into their midst, saluted the

---

* The last phrase, according to old custom, has to be uttered by both attendants at the same time. All these ceremonial observances can still be studied on the Japanese stage.

† This was the name given to the estrade, or dais, upon which a feudal prince or ruler sat in state. The term literally signifies "great seat."

king with the triple prostration of usage. The king greeted him with gracious words, and then said:—

"You have already been informed as to the reason of your having been summoned to Our presence. We have decided that you shall become the adopted husband of Our only daughter;—and the wedding ceremony shall now be performed."

As the king finished speaking, a sound of joyful music was heard; and a long train of beautiful court ladies advanced from behind a curtain to conduct Akinosuké to the room in which his bride awaited him.

The room was immense; but it could scarcely contain the multitude of guests assembled to witness the wedding ceremony. All bowed down before Akinosuké as he took his place, facing the King's daughter, on the kneeling-cushion prepared for him. As a maiden of heaven the bride appeared to be; and her robes were beautiful as a summer sky. And the marriage was performed amid great rejoicing.

Afterwards the pair were conducted to a suite of apartments that had been prepared for them in another portion of the palace; and there they received the congratulations of many noble persons, and wedding gifts beyond counting.

Some days later Akinosuké was again summoned to the throne-room. On this occasion he was received even more graciously than before; and the King said to him:—

"In the southwestern part of Our dominion there is an island called Raishū. We have now appointed you Governor of that island. You will find the people loyal and docile; but their laws have not yet been brought into proper accord with the laws of Tokoyo; and their customs have not been properly regulated. We entrust you with the duty of improving their social condition as far as may be possible; and We desire that you shall rule them with kindness and wisdom. All preparations necessary for your journey to Raishū have already been made."

So Akinosuké and his bride departed from the palace of To-koyo, accompanied to the shore by a great escort of nobles and officials; and they embarked upon a ship of state provided by the king. And with favoring winds they safety sailed to Raishū, and found the good people of that island assembled upon the beach to welcome them.

Akinosuké entered at once upon his new duties; and they did not prove to be hard. During the first three years of his governor-ship he was occupied chiefly with the framing and the enactment of laws; but he had wise counselors to help him, and he never found the work unpleasant.

When it was all finished, he had no active duties to perform, beyond attending the rites and ceremonies ordained by ancient custom. The country was so healthy and so fertile that sickness and want were unknown; and the people were so good that no laws were ever broken. And Akinosuké dwelt and ruled in Raishū for twenty years more,—making in all twenty-three years of sojourn, during which no shadow of sorrow traversed his life.

But in the twenty-fourth year of his governorship, a great mis-fortune came upon him; for his wife, who had borne him seven children,—five boys and two girls,—fell sick and died. She was buried, with high pomp, on the summit of a beautiful hill in the district of Hanryōkō; and a monument, exceedingly splendid, was placed upon her grave. But Akinosuké felt such grief at her death that he no longer cared to live.

Now when the legal period of mourning was over, there came to Raishū, from the Tokoyo palace, a *shisha*, or royal messenger.

The shisha delivered to Akinosuké a message of condolence, and then said to him:—

"These are the words which our august master, the King of Tokoyo, commands that I repeat to you: 'We will now send you back to your own people and country. As for the seven children, they are the grandsons and granddaughters of the King, and shall be fitly cared for. Do not, therefore, allow your mind to be troubled concerning them.'"

On receiving this mandate, Akinosuké submissively prepared for his departure. When all his affairs had been settled, and the ceremony of bidding farewell to his counselors and trusted officials had been concluded, he was escorted with much honor to the port. There he embarked upon the ship sent for him; and the ship sailed out into the blue sea, under the blue sky; and the shape of the island of Raishū itself turned blue, and then turned gray, and then vanished forever. . . . And Akinosuké suddenly awoke—under the cedar-tree in his own garden!

For a moment he was stupefied and dazed. But he perceived his two friends still seated near him,—drinking and chatting merrily. He stared at them in a bewildered way, and cried aloud,—

"How strange!"

"Akinosuké must have been dreaming," one of them exclaimed, with a laugh. "What did you see, Akinosuké, that was strange?"

Then Akinosuké told his dream,—that dream of three-and-twenty years' sojourn in the realm of Tokoyo, in the island of Raishū;—and they were astonished, because he had really slept for no more than a few minutes.

One gōshi said:—

"Indeed, you saw strange things. We also saw something strange while you were napping. A little yellow butterfly was fluttering over your face for a moment or two; and we watched it. Then it alighted on the ground beside you, close to the tree; and almost as soon as it alighted there, a big, big ant came out of a hole and seized it and pulled it down into the hole. Just before you woke up, we saw that very butterfly come out of the hole again, and flutter over your face as before. And then it suddenly disappeared: we do not know where it went."

"Perhaps it was Akinosuké's soul," the other gōshi said;— "certainly I thought I saw it fly into his mouth. . . . But, even if that butterfly was Akinosuké's soul, the fact would not explain his dream."

"The ants might explain it," returned the first speaker. "Ants are queer beings—possibly goblins. . . . Anyhow, there is a big ant's nest under that cedar-tree. . . ."

"Let us look!" cried Akinosuké, greatly moved by this suggestion. And he went for a spade.

The ground about and beneath the cedar-tree proved to have been excavated, in a most surprising way, by a prodigious colony of ants. The ants had furthermore built inside their excavations; and their tiny constructions of straw, clay, and stems bore an odd resemblance to miniature towns. In the middle of a structure considerably larger than the rest there was a marvelous swarming of small ants around the body of one very big ant, which had yellowish wings and a long black head.

"Why, there is the King of my dream!" cried Akinosuké; "and there is the palace of Tokoyo! . . . How extraordinary! . . . Raishū ought to lie somewhere southwest of it—to the left of that big root. . . . Yes!—here it is! . . . How very strange! Now I am sure that I can find the mountain of Hanryōkō, and the grave of the princess. . . ."

In the wreck of the nest he searched and searched, and at last discovered a tiny mound, on the top of which was fixed a water-worn pebble, in shape resembling a Buddhist monument. Underneath it he found—embedded in clay—the dead body of a female ant.

His name was Riki, signifying Strength; but the people called him Riki-the-Simple, or Riki-the-Fool,—"Riki-Baka,"—because he had been born into perpetual childhood. For the same reason they were kind to him,—even when he set a house on fire by putting a lighted match to a mosquito-curtain, and clapped his hands for joy to see the blaze. At sixteen years he was a tall, strong lad; but in mind he remained always at the happy age of two, and therefore continued to play with very small children. The bigger children of the neighborhood, from four to seven years old, did not care to play with him, because he could not learn their songs and games. His favorite toy was a broomstick, which he used as a hobby-horse; and for hours at a time he would ride on that broomstick, up and down the slope in front of my house, with amazing peals of laughter. But at last he became troublesome by reason of his noise; and I had to tell him that he must find another playground. He bowed submissively, and then went off,—sorrowfully trailing his broomstick behind him. Gentle at all times, and perfectly harmless if allowed no chance to play with fire, he seldom gave anybody cause for complaint. His relation to the life of our street was scarcely more than that of a dog or a chicken; and when he finally disappeared, I did not miss him. Months and months passed by before anything happened to remind me of Riki.

"What has become of Riki?" I then asked the old woodcutter who supplies our neighborhood with fuel. I remembered that Riki had often helped him to carry his bundles.

"Riki-Baka?" answered the old man. "Ah, Riki is dead—poor fellow! . . . Yes, he died nearly a year ago, very suddenly; the doctors said that he had some disease of the brain. And there is a strange story now about that poor Riki.

"When Riki died, his mother wrote his name, 'Riki-Baka,' in the palm of his left hand,—putting 'Riki' in the Chinese character, and 'Baka' in *kana*. And she repeated many prayers for him,—prayers that he might be reborn into some more happy condition.

"Now, about three months ago, in the honorable residence of Nanigashi-Sama, in Kōjimachi, a boy was born with characters on the palm of his left hand; and the characters were quite plain to read,—'*RIKI-BAKA*'!

"So the people of that house knew that the birth must have happened in answer to somebody's prayer; and they caused inquiry to be made everywhere. At last a vegetable-seller brought word to them that there used to be a simple lad, called Riki-Baka, living in the Ushigomé quarter, and that he had died during the last autumn; and they sent two men-servants to look for the mother of Riki.

"Those servants found the mother of Riki, and told her what had happened; and she was glad exceedingly—for that Nanigashi house is a very rich and famous house. But the servants said that the family of Nanigashi-Sama were very angry about the word 'Baka' on the child's hand. 'And where is your Riki buried?' the servants asked. 'He is buried in the cemetery of Zendōji,' she told them. 'Please to give us some of the clay of his grave,' they requested.

"So she went with them to the temple Zendōji, and showed them Riki's grave; and they took some of the grave-clay away with them, wrapped up in a *furoshiki*.*. . . . They gave Riki's mother some money,—ten yen. . . ."

"But what did they want with that clay?" I inquired.

"Well," the old man answered, "you know that it would not do to let the child grow up with that name on his hand. And there is no other means of removing characters that come in that way upon the body of a child: *you must rub the skin with clay taken from the grave of the body of the former birth. . . .*"

---

* A square piece of cotton-goods, or other woven material, used as a wrap in which to carry small packages.

On the wooded hill behind the house Robert and I are looking for fairy-rings. Robert is eight years old, comely, and very wise;—I am a little more than seven,—and I reverence Robert. It is a glowing glorious August day; and the warm air is filled with sharp sweet scents of resin.

We do not find any fairy-rings; but we find a great many pine-cones in the high grass. . . . I tell Robert the old Welsh story of the man who went to sleep, unawares, inside a fairy-ring, and so disappeared for seven years, and would never eat or speak after his friends had delivered him from the enchantment.

"They eat nothing but the points of needles, you know," says Robert.

"Who?" I ask.

"Goblins," Robert answers.

This revelation leaves me dumb with astonishment and awe. . . . But Robert suddenly cries out:—

"There is a Harper!—he is coming to the house!"

And down the hill we run to hear the harper. . . . But what a harper! Not like the hoary minstrels of the picture-books. A swarthy, sturdy, unkempt vagabond, with black bold eyes under scowling black brows. More like a bricklayer than a bard,—and his garments are corduroy!

"Wonder if he is going to sing in Welsh?" murmurs Robert.

I feel too much disappointed to make any remarks. The harper poses his harp—a huge instrument—upon our doorstep, sets all the strings ringing with a sweep of his grimy fingers, clears his throat with a sort of angry growl, and begins,—

> Believe me, if all those endearing young charms,
> Which I gaze on so fondly today. . . .

The accent, the attitude, the voice, all fill me with repulsion unutterable,—shock me with a new sensation of formidable vulgarity. I want to cry out loud, "You have no right to sing that song!" For I have heard it sung by the lips of the dearest and fairest being in my little world;—and that this rude, coarse man should dare to sing it vexes me like a mockery,—angers me like an insolence. But only for a moment! . . . With the utterance of the syllables "today," that deep, grim voice suddenly breaks into a quivering tenderness indescribable;—then, marvelously changing, it mellows into tones sonorous and rich as the bass of a great organ,—while a sensation unlike anything ever felt before takes me by the throat. . . . What witchcraft has he learned? What secret has he found—this scowling man of the road? . . . Oh! is there anybody else in the whole world who can sing like that? . . . And the form of the singer flickers and dims;—and the house, and the lawn, and all visible shapes of things tremble and swim before me. Yet instinctively I fear that man;—I almost hate him; and I feel myself flushing with anger and shame because of his power to move me thus. . . .

"He made you cry," Robert compassionately observes, to my further confusion,—as the harper strides away, richer by a gift of sixpence taken without thanks. . . . "But I think he must be a gipsy.

Gipsies are bad people—and they are wizards. . . . Let us go back to the wood."

We climb again to the pines, and there squat down upon the sun-flecked grass, and look over town and sea. But we do not play as before: the spell of the wizard is strong upon us both. . . . "Perhaps he is a goblin," I venture at last, "or a fairy?" "No," says Robert,—"only a gipsy. But that is nearly as bad. They steal children, you know. . . ."

"What shall we do if he comes up here?" I gasp, in sudden terror at the lonesomeness of our situation.

"Oh, he wouldn't dare," answers Robert—"not by daylight, you know. . . ."

(Only yesterday, near the village of Takata, I noticed a flower which the Japanese call by nearly the same name as we do: *Himawari*, "The Sunward-turning";—and over the space of forty years there thrilled back to me the voice of that wandering harper,—

As the Sunflower turns on her god, when he sets,
The same look that she turned when he rose.

Again I saw the sun-flecked shadows on that far Welsh hill; and Robert for a moment again stood beside me, with his girl's face and his curls of gold. We were looking for fairy-rings. . . . But all that existed of the real Robert must long ago have suffered a sea-change into something rich and strange. . . . *Greater love hath no man than this, that a man lay down his life for his friend. . . .*)

Blue vision of depth lost in height,—sea and sky interblending through luminous haze. The day is of spring, and the hour morning.

Only sky and sea,—one azure enormity. . . . In the fore, ripples are catching a silvery light, and threads of foam are swirling. But a little further off no motion is visible, nor anything save color: dim warm blue of water widening away to melt into blue of air. Horizon there is none: only distance soaring into space,—infinite concavity hollowing before you, and hugely arching above you,—the color deepening with the height. But far in the midway-blue there hangs a faint, faint vision of palace towers, with high roofs horned and curved like moons,—some shadowing of splendor strange and old, illumined by a sunshine soft as memory.

. . . What I have thus been trying to describe is a kakémono,— that is to say, a Japanese painting on silk, suspended to the wall of my alcove;—and the name of it is Shinkirō, which signifies "Mirage." But the shapes of the mirage are unmistakable. Those are the glimmering portals of Hōrai the blest; and those are the moony roofs of the Palace of the Dragon-King;—and the fashion of them (though limned by a Japanese brush of today) is the fashion of things Chinese, twenty-one hundred years ago. . . .

Thus much is told of the place in the Chinese books of that time:—

In Hōrai there is neither death nor pain; and there is no winter. The flowers in that place never fade, and the fruits never fail; and if a man taste of those fruits even but once, he can never again feel thirst or hunger. In Hōrai grow the enchanted plants *So-rin-shi*, and *Riku-gō-aoi*, and *Ban-kon-tō*, which heal all manner of sickness;—and there grows also the magical grass *Yo-shin-shi*, that quickens the dead; and the magical grass is watered by a fairy water of which a single drink confers perpetual youth. The people of Hōrai eat their rice out of very, very small bowls; but the rice never diminishes within those bowls,—however much of it be eaten,—until the eater desires no more. And the people of Hōrai drink their wine out of very, very small cups; but no man can empty one of those cups,—however stoutly he may drink,—until there comes upon him the pleasant drowsiness of intoxication.

All this and more is told in the legends of the time of the Shin dynasty. But that the people who wrote down those legends ever saw Hōrai, even in a mirage, is not believable. For really there are no enchanted fruits which leave the eater forever satisfied,—nor any magical grass which revives the dead,—nor any fountain of fairy water,—nor any bowls which never lack rice,—nor any cups which never lack wine. It is not true that sorrow and death never enter Hōrai;—neither is it true that there is not any winter. The winter in Hōrai is cold;—and winds then bite to the bone; and the heaping of snow is monstrous on the roofs of the Dragon-King.

Nevertheless there are wonderful things in Hōrai; and the most wonderful of all has not been mentioned by any Chinese writer. I mean the atmosphere of Hōrai. It is an atmosphere peculiar to the place; and, because of it, the sunshine in Hōrai is *whiter* than any other sunshine,—a milky light that never dazzles,—astonishingly clear, but very soft. This atmosphere is not of our human period:

it is enormously old,—so old that I feel afraid when I try to think how old it is;—and it is not a mixture of nitrogen and oxygen. It is not made of air at all, but of ghost,—the substance of quintillions of quintillions of generations of souls blended into one immense translucency,—souls of people who thought in ways never resembling our ways. Whatever mortal man inhales that atmosphere, he takes into his blood the thrilling of these spirits; and they change the sense within him,—reshaping his notions of Space and Time,—so that he can see only as they used to see, and feel only as they used to feel, and think only as they used to think. Soft as sleep are these changes of sense; and Hōrai, discerned across them, might thus be described:—

—Because in Hōrai there is no knowledge of great evil, the hearts of the people never grow old. And, by reason of being always young in heart, the people of Hōrai smile from birth until death—except when the Gods send sorrow among them; and faces then are veiled until the sorrow goes away. All folk in Hōrai love and trust each other, as if all were members of a single household;—and the speech of the women is like birdsong, because the hearts of them are light as the souls of birds;—and the swaying of the sleeves of the maidens at play seems a flutter of wide, soft wings. In Hōrai nothing is hidden but grief, because there is no reason for shame;—and nothing is locked away, because there could not be any theft;—and by night as well as by day all doors remain unbarred, because there is no reason for fear. And because the people are fairies—though mortal—all things in Hōrai, except the Palace of the Dragon-King, are small and quaint and queer;—and these fairy-folk do really eat their rice out of very, very small bowls, and drink their wine out of very, very small cups. . . .

—Much of this seemingly would be due to the inhalation of that ghostly atmosphere—but not all. For the spell wrought by the dead is only the charm of an Ideal, the glamour of an ancient hope;—and something of that hope has found fulfillment in many hearts,—in the simple beauty of unselfish lives,—in the sweetness of Woman. . . .

—Evil winds from the West are blowing over Hōrai; and the magical atmosphere, alas! is shrinking away before them. It lingers now in patches only, and bands,—like those long bright bands of cloud that train across the landscapes of Japanese painters. Under these shreds of the elfish vapor you still can find Hōrai—but not everywhere. . . . Remember that Hōrai is also called Shinkirō, which signifies Mirage,—the Vision of the Intangible. And the Vision is fading,—never again to appear save in pictures and poems and dreams. . . .

Amenomori, Nobushige. "Lafcadio Hearn, the Man." *Atlantic Monthly* (October 1905): 510–524.

Bisland, Elizabeth. *The Life and Letters of Lafcadio Hearn.* 2 vols. Boston: Houghton Mifflin, 1906.

Bronner, Simon. "'Gombo' Folkloristics: Lafcadio Hearn's Creolization and Hybridization in the Formative Period of Folklore Studies." *Journal of Folklore Research* 12/2 (2005): 141–184.

Cott, Jonathan. *Wandering Ghost: The Odyssey of Lafcadio Hearn.* Tokyo: Kodansha International, 1992.

Cowley, Malcolm. "Lafcadio Hearn." In *The Selected Writings of Lafcadio Hearn.* Ed. H Goodman. New York: Citadel Press, 1949, 1–15.

Dawson, Carl. *Lafcadio Hearn and the Vision of Japan.* Baltimore, MD: Johns Hopkins University Press, 1992.

Gould, George M. *Concerning Lafcadio Hearn.* Philadelphia: George W. Jacobs, 1908.

Kennard, Nina H. *Lafcadio Hearn.* New York: D. Appleton, 1912.

Kunst, Arthur E. *Lafcadio Hearn.* New York: Twayne, 1969.

Langton, D. H. "Lafcadio Hearn: Journalist and Writer on Japan." *Manchester Quarterly* 31 (1912): 1–23.

Lee, Mabel, and A. D. Stefanowska. *Literary Intercrossings: East Asia and the West.* Sydney, Australia: Wild Peony, 1998.

McWilliams, Vera. *Lafcadio Hearn.* New York: Houghton Mifflin, 1946.

Miner, Earl Roy. *The Japanese Tradition in British and American Literature.* Princeton, NJ: Princeton University Press, 1958.

Ota, Yuzo. "Lafcadio Hearn's Stories Based on Japanese Sources." In *Literary Intercrossings: East Asia and the West*. Eds. Mabel Lee and A. D. Stefanowska. Sydney, Australia: Wild Peony, 1998, 122–127.

Pulvers, Roger. "Lafcadio Hearn: Interpreter of Two Disparate Worlds." *Japan Times* (January 19, 2000); available at www.trussel.com/hearn/pulvers.htm (accessed September 14, 2017).

Rexroth, Kenneth. *The Buddhist Writings of Lafcadio Hearn*. Santa Barbara, CA: Ross-Erikson, 1977.

Setsu, Koizumi. *Reminiscences of Lafcadio Hearn*. New York: Houghton Mifflin, 1918.